Amy.

I wish this book will give you access to a life filled with love.

♡ Sophie .

The
ELEGANCE
OF
SIMPLICITY

The
ELEGANCE
OF
SIMPLICITY

A Wisdom Teacher's Epic Journey to Awareness

Sophie McLean

A PRAYER

I wish to make a deal with you.

I will tell you all.

I will bare it all.

I will be the provocateur.

I will take you out of your comfort zone.

I will guide you beyond the limits of your thinking.

I will even give you answers you understand.

In return, I ask only one thing:

Throw off the unbearable weight of the habitual for the pursuit of the extraordinary.

For the sake of humankind.

Murray,

Mon Cœur,

Forever and beyond.

There are certain things you can only know by creating
them for yourself.

ACKNOWLEDGMENTS

To the myriad of people that have contributed to me:

Lamia, my dear friend

My 'crew+ team', Misha, Donna, Karen, Stephanie and Boaz

My family

My friends

My many students and my many masters

Please let these few lines reach deep into your hearts and allow yourselves to experience my profound gratitude.

TABLE OF CONTENTS

TABLE OF CONTENTS

TABLE OF CONTENTS

PROLOGUE

I would have liked so much to be able to write a book beginning with, "Once upon a time, there was a marvelous and beautiful princess," which would recount the bliss of a life filled with ease and grace. My journey led me somewhere else, though, far away from fairy tales. Yet, in a mocking paradox I did not foresee, the outcome was to become my own miracle. It happened in an unexpected way, in a dimension where my discovery would exceed my wildest dreams.

I was a woman imprisoned in an ordinary and comfortable existence made up of heartbreak and routine, misunderstandings and mundane nights, work and entertainment—a life that was certainly acceptable, but whose lack of passion and meaning suffocated me. At thirty- five years of age, already divorced without children, I worked as a professor of political science at a prestigious university in Paris. I was a dainty-looking woman with short, curly hair, and my small size and delicate features allowed me to outsmart more than one naïve person who mistook my lack of physical stature for a lack of power. There is something to be said for gracile appearances!

Being French and living in France allowed me many advantages, one of which was a quality of life unequaled in the rest of the world. France, the country of human rights, with its motto of "liberty, equality, fraternity," has always looked after its citizens, sometimes far too much. We drift toward a culture of demanding, victimized people who are afraid to lose the privileges gained through the grassroots movements in our history. My compatriots were always capable of the best and the worst, and I loved them for it, being myself a product of that same culture.

Our favorite pastime was talking endlessly about life. I never knew if our affinity for long, delicious meals came from the need to create a setting for existential conversations, or if those conversations gave birth to our culinary expertise. Whatever the case, French people can talk. And think. And criticize. And take a stand, when the need arises.

I had a busy social and professional schedule that led me to participate in myriad conversations about what to do, say, change, or destroy in our world to make it more equitable for everyone. Of course, these ideas came from individuals who thought they had the solutions to all the misfortunes of humanity, never considering that their solutions were, in fact, new versions of the problem. In all likelihood, moving forward with these interventions would merely lead to a trap similar to the one in which human beings have struggled since the time of Homer and his *Iliad*.

I heard the good intentions behind these ideas, shared them, even. But I could not fail to notice that my compatriots allowed themselves opinions and offered advice without any investment on their part. I strongly suspected that if my friends were one day in charge of society, these problems would remain. Their relentless criticism of others, who were always wrong and who were to be blamed for all ills, convinced me that the world was the way it was because of all of us.

At some point, I began to fall silent during these conversations, having lost the courage to endure the sarcasm and accusations of stupidity that burst forth as soon as I expressed my deviant point of view. They could not agree with my belief that only a transformation of our beingness—the state in which we exist—could allow us to create a world that would work for everyone.

One day, abruptly, in a desperate gesture, I decided to escape my agreeable routine, which was becoming less enjoyable by the day. I threw myself into a quest driven by the irrepressible thought that something had to give. I wanted answers. I wanted to find out the meaning of life.

I sold my apartment, gave away my furniture, gifted my delighted girlfriends my designer clothes, and with only a backpack and my passport, I left my life to discover the world. Behind me trailed the shouts of friends and family, warning me of the terrible dangers a single woman would certainly encounter on such a foolish enterprise, and predicting my demise.

I wandered around the world for five years, experiencing highs and lows, unwilling to go back to the familiar life I had left until I found the answers to my questions. The day I met Guìa, the woman whose story I will tell, was my moment of truth. Hers was a typical, difficult life that exploded into the extraordinary; a life which made possible the amazing, the exceptional, the impossible, even the improbable. Sometimes, in looking back, I wonder what my life would have been like if I had not recognized its significance. But I did, and that is what matters.

I encountered Guìa during my travels to an African coast, where the inhabitants of a small village welcomed me for a few months. They accepted me into their community with an absence of curiosity or questions. I could not have told them much anyhow, not knowing myself how to formulate the purpose of my journey.

After a few months of sharing their field work during the day, and listening to their stories at night while gathered around the village's central fire, they told me what I first thought was the legend of their people. I later discovered it was not at all a legend, but simply a different and unqualified reality. The villagers never tried to convince me of the truth of what they confided. They spoke to me with simplicity, as one describes the obvious, without the need to persuade.

They told me that they were protected by an eminently wise woman named Guìa, who visited them from time to time. She lived in a small house by the sea, but no one could tell me where, because she, alone, chose those who were able to find their way to her. The path was revealed only if and when it was needed. That was all they would say about her. In spite of my insistence, no one was willing to share their personal experience of this woman, nor the miracles she performed, nor the benefits that were generated from her presence. My mind took hold of this legend with as much doggedness as a thirsty person looking for water after crossing the desert, and I never stopped searching for her until I met her.

I spent weeks praying and wandering the African countryside and deserted beaches, inexplicably certain of the wise woman's existence. I am now convinced that this very lack of doubt is what ultimately led me to her. One day, suddenly, she was in front of me, silent and smiling. Then she told me she was Guìa, and she offered to talk—if I would do something for her, in return.

She asked me to write her story. She made me promise to tell everything because, she said, newcomers to life needed a guidebook, so they could learn faster. It was high time, she added, for humanity to awaken.

Her story belongs to all of us, men and women who are called to live for a time on our Earth. Her story is that of human beings since the beginning of time, with their concerns, their hopes, and their battles. Her story is about the miracle of creation.

PART I

THE UNIVERSAL
AT PLAY

CHAPTER 1

THE COVENANT

One moment I am walking, lost in my thoughts, and the next, Guìa is there, standing in the middle of a sandy path not far from the village I live in. I stop, not knowing what to say. After all, what can I say? *Are you the woman who performs miracles?* Or, even worse, *Are you real?*

I stay silent, waiting for her to take the lead. Her first move is a smile. The second, still without a word, is to take me by the hand and lead me gently along the trail toward the seashore. Then she tells me who she is, and we arrive at a pact—an exchange of services—to which I agree, without knowing why.

It is impossible for me to assess her age. Guìa is striking in an unconventional way, with abundant hair, fine hands, a body of adorable grace without any insipid cuteness, and skin the color of ripe, golden fruit. She is wearing a simple, white dress. I especially notice her eyes; I have a feeling those eyes will never leave me and will be imprinted on my soul from this moment. Eyes that are bottomless and forever. Eyes that reflect what I do not know how to qualify, but which I sense are full of wonder and joy.

And she is barefoot.

We arrive on her home beach, and I discover a small fisherman's house of white wood, simple and clean. Its roof slants softly, and windows frame two sides of a painted blue door, a blue so vibrant it dances with the sunlight. Two empty armchairs beckon from a veranda made of planks lying directly on the ground; it is sheltered by coconut branches. I can imagine spending blissful hours sitting here, enjoying the sight of the sparkling sea lined with the velvet of a fine sand.

We sit. I am already in wonder at her presence, and I wait without impatience for her good will, surprised that all my questions have disappeared. After a long silence, Guìa begins to speak to me, without preamble or explanation, her voice both sweet and powerful.

> *The vastness is weightless and transparent. It is made of soft and bluish waves of light, vaporous and diaphanous, which gently undulate toward forever and beyond. The infinity of love, and the beauty that emerges with it, stretch out, like lovers would after having known the bliss of an embrace. The eternal is forever luminous. Its luster is fully self-sufficient and is never qualified by what it illuminates: the brightness is revealed to itself and manifests the surroundings, yet the revealed surroundings have no impact on the immutable.*

I understand she is talking about a world beyond my reality, and I listen, at a loss for words, when she tells me the radiant presence of souls is of the same nature.

Souls are in nonidentification, in pure knowledge, in emptiness, in the ultimate, nondual, brilliant presence of consciousness: a pure and fundamental presence without any particular determination, except for an individuality without separation, a communion without disappearance. This consciousness is a mirror that reflects itself. This consciousness is a lamp that illuminates the infinite without being it, but by being of it. This consciousness is pure possibility.

I accept that she is speaking of an extraterrestrial reality, and I hold my breath, not wanting to interrupt her monologue, which already has begun to address my desire for answers. Guìa seems to speak to my most instinctive wish by sharing the secrets of the infinite. That I do not fully grasp what she is saying does not matter. I intuit her meaning. And above all, I have hope.

She describes herself as a body without any outline, a medley of veils of light embellished by an immaterial existence. Guìa illustrates herself as a soft, numinous, and ethereal consciousness, an awareness that can create many different states, in the manner that water takes the form of ice, rain, clouds, rivers, or seas.

She tells me that, before coming to Earth, she inhabited a kind of sanctuary created as, or from, an image of her soul. From what I can gather, this sanctuary is the way nature could be if neither time nor weather influenced the growing of plants or the living of animals. Everything was only and always a reflection of herself.

She speaks of birds of a thousand colors, graceful butterflies, and white rabbits. She speaks of goats, mischievous marmosets, and cows with big, romantic eyes and of meerkats, many meerkats, intelligent, curious, and kind. She says she liked them most. She also had lions. Guìa tells me that she was always surrounded and followed by her felines, Quirinus and Anvil. She loved, she says, to lie down with them at the foot of a majestic, silver weeping willow and watch the games of the other animals.

She describes to me a river, gentle hills, beautiful trees—and flowers, flowers, and more flowers. Roses with exquisite aroma and petals celebrating beauty; chubby anemones with resplendent colors; bright and generous peonies and lantana, reflecting the stars. She speaks of hydrangeas with the movement of fireworks, and white daisies that expressed the elegance of simplicity. The floor she walked on was like a soft quilt sprinkled with dewlike drops of light.

I cannot report her exact words because she does not speak a language I am familiar with, and yet I understand her perfectly. Her descriptions remind me of Earth's flowers, our animals, and our world, so I layer my familiar words over her narrative.

She says that throughout the infinite, all eternal expressions of divine energy are possible and are created out of nothing. I realize she has the power to manifest what she wishes.

There are wise souls, masters, creators, players, and lovers. There are fairies, goblins, and dragons. There is beauty, generosity, love, and joy. There are angels, guides, and leprechauns. There is what I create. I am God inside of God.

Guìa presents herself as the guardian of feminine wisdom, guiding others to eternal tenderness. She also tells me of Mathusial, an oracle of immense authority in the world she painted for me. He is the Master of Directions, the expression of order and harmony, and his mission is to support the incarnation of souls on Earth. There are, apparently, several places and many forms of incarnation in the divine infinite, but Mathusial is in charge of Earth, the most difficult place of embodiment, the one reserved for advanced souls.

Guìa then startles me by stating, without any warning, that the point of our incarnation is to experience survival. Her use of the word "survival"—in our language of mutual understanding—astonishes me, and despite my intent to remain silent, I insist on knowing the reason for her choice. She patiently explains it to me.

> *When we are confronted with danger, or when we think something threatens us, we need to protect ourselves. Think of being the target of a predator. You will look for a means to survive, either by hiding, running, or attacking. For human beings, most of what happens in life is a threat. And for protection, we form a defensive, armor-clad, virtual cage around ourselves. That cage is called the ego. The ego has many facets, but each is designed with a single, focused intention: to survive. The ego is like a prison, because it limits our ontological freedom—our freedom to be. Our Self, our soul, and our body are strangled and jailed by this shell. When our ego is the source of our thoughts, our actions, and the results we produce, we are not.*

I am not sure I understand her depiction. Is she telling me the purpose of this earthly incarnation is to survive—as in, to not to die from—a danger? The questions jostle in my head, but a particular one screams with indignation more loudly than all others, burning my lips. Before I can cry out in desperate protest, Guìa laughs as if she has heard my internal revolt, and she simply answers it.

> *It is necessary to survive in order to remember it is possible to live.*

Her eyes sparkle with mischief, teasing and joyful like the fairy I now imagine her to be. She has defused my explosion with an existential pirouette, knowing I will not understand all of her words. But she has allowed me to catch my breath and enabled me to listen anew. She continues.

> *We live when our Self, or our soul, if you prefer, is at the source of our thoughts, our actions, and, therefore, the results we produce. To live implies a deep acceptance of what is happening and what we are feeling. We live when we are conscious that the apparent threat is only an illusion.*

She adds an allegory.

> *In this dimension, life can be compared to an ocean, with its waves and storms, with its calm and tranquility, its sunrises and sunsets. Imagine people as surfers on the waves of life. Our surfboard is our life, and we will have it until our death. If we do not manage to take one wave into shore, another will always follow and carry us in. Storms pass, just like the good*

weather. The cycle is endless. The experience of being alive is an adventure, and when we accept it, we enter the presence of the irresistible, which opens us up to gratitude and wonder. We are one with nature.

I do not want to rudely express my doubts, but life is, indeed, filled with danger! And it is all very well to be one with nature, but a person has to be realistic. Like a coward, I stay quiet.

She reminds me that only advanced souls come for a stay on Planet Earth, as it is a challenging endeavor. Human beings' power of creation allows them to choose between survival and living, and this is, according to her, the grace of this incarnation, as well as its difficulty.

She closes her eyes while sharing this, smiling mysteriously. Though I do not know what this woman sees, in the moment of now I can sense that her smile bears the imprint of millennia of unconscious survival, with their horror and violence in the abyss of human despair, as well as her recognition of the redemption of awakening.

She carries on.

The difficulty of incarnation on Earth arises because of the rule of the human game. Every incarnation must forget its divinity very soon after its arrival in the body. But at the very time divinity is forgotten, the soul forgets the golden rule of the universe: the harvest is always in perfect correlation with what has been sown.

The universe is in total integrity with the all, and the harmony is always perfect. Everything is created, and nothing is lost. The duality engendered by the forgetting of one's own divinity brings an intense suffering to the soul, and this deep misery will not disappear until the awakening.

The worst of noneternal pain is the sensation of separation experienced by humans. Having forgotten we are a material expressions of the divine, we feel alone and abandoned. Fear floods our living space like a viscous, dark liquid, claiming all interstices. Fear dominates, and we are left only with the option to identify with what is observable, such as our bodies, our personalities, our character, our thoughts, our emotions, and the circumstances of the world we think we see. We are then deprived of consciousness—stifled, uprooted, and left gasping for breath.

I feel terrified by her words, which describe the world I have been struggling with. I am not sure I want her to continue, but she ignores my resistance and proceeds with her account.

This suffering must lead humans to remember who they really are, and to never again forget their divinity. This is the game of life. We must move from survival to living before we can return home.

I breathe a little easier, yet I am disrupted and shaken to the depths of my being. She has to know it, because she tells me it is time for me to leave her.

I worry that I won't find my way back to her little house the next day, but she gently tells me that I have to come back. So, I know I will. I return slowly to the village, absorbed by my thoughts, which are in full disorder. I recall that someone once told me to be careful what I wish for, and I am now uneasy about where this encounter will lead me. Should I run?

In the end, what makes me stick with Guìa is that she seems to be connected to all that exists. Love radiates from her. In an effort to quiet my mind, I tell myself I have been looking for soul consciousness, for awareness, and I cannot run away at the very moment my intention seems on the verge of being fulfilled. After all, that is what miracles are: the instant realization of one's intention.

CHAPTER 2

THE BOUDOIR

I return the next day, finding my way easily, and I see Guìa sitting in one of the two chairs I have already come to consider my thrones of consciousness. She greets me with her beautiful, sunny smile and continues at once with her story.

> *Mathusial must help human beings live. He has at his disposal various options to support them, but nothing can undermine the free will of human beings. They must make their way and learn through the experiences life presents to them. The golden arrow in Mathusial's quiver is inspiration. Only inspiration can encourage people to listen, think, and remember their divinity. Inspiration is the consecrated breath, par excellence. It is also sometimes called intuition, and it alone can interrupt the call of destruction and fear. To fulfill their mission, humans must learn to listen to the universe.*

The rules Guia sets for our meetings are simple, if not easy. I should not seek answers. I should not use my knowledge or my intellect to understand what she is communicating. My duty is to listen, both to her and to my Self.

Leaning forward to give more weight to her words, she continues.

> *The twenty-first century is a chance for sentient beings. They will finally have the opportunity to rise through their incarnation and achieve the profound experience of being a divine expression. The time has come.*

I do not know what to think of the underlying urgency of her words, and I choose once more to remain silent, comprehending as good news my inability to formulate a thought. There are times when words are too small, too limited, and I know something is penetrating my being. She inculcates her message beyond understanding, beyond logic and deduction, beyond conscious thought.

She continues.

> *To that effect, one of Mathusial's resources is to send his most magnificent workforce to Earth; these are karma's guardians. These souls have already accomplished their elevation and returned to the infinite, leaving earthly survival far behind. However, when Mathusial asks them to contribute, they respond to a new call of incarnation without hesitation or even deliberation. In the eternal, the sharing is complete and the altruism profound.*

Guìa tells me she was one of those souls who did not have to come back, other than for a specific mission; she returned to our world willingly. She is joyful in relaying this, as if stating, *mission accomplished.* She seems to delight in a secret that she alone can hear, and she finds my perplexity charming.

She begins the story of her incarnation by describing the moment she chose to return to Earth.

> *Mathusial asked me if I would go back to Earth for a life. I asked him what my mission would be, and he told me I had to presence Grace, the unmerited love of God for mankind. I tried to bargain, asking whether I could keep my soul memory of the divine, but he flatly refused, because the rules are immutable.*

Once Guìa accepted Mathusial's request, the passage from wholeness to duality became inevitable. The test of forgetfulness was unavoidable.

I learn that there is one entry point into our world, and Guìa describes it as a bright and always accessible corridor between the heavenly and earthly dimensions, although she insists there is no distance between the two. Souls float easily and gracefully from one dimension to the other, in either direction. As long as the souls retain the memory of the divine, they can do this at will. Only forgetfulness, the ultimate test, precludes them from changing planes.

I am like a child listening to the most beautiful fairy tale, imagining a magical path where non-incarnated souls float. Guìa describes her experience of going back and forth between the celestial and the terrestrial worlds. Having said earlier that, like every one of us, she had to forget who she really was, her ability to relate the process of incarnation to me now stirs a whirlwind of hope. She has remembered, and maybe, so can I.

She describes when her mother was carrying her little body in the process of forming, and like all babies in the making, Guìa's soul had to take time to get used to the body that was intended for her. To allow for this, she lived the nine months of her mother's pregnancy by intermittently moving between the two planes, physical and ethereal, with the periods of incarnation getting longer and longer as her birth time drew closer.

> *It is difficult for souls to be confined to a body, subject to the laws of gravity and time. The body has to become an expression and a majestic reflection of the divine, so the period of habituation that pregnancy allows is necessary. The experience of being alive begins in this timeless phase between the two dimensions.*

Guìa should have experienced freedom and delight as she started her life, since she still remembered her divinity and was in deep acceptance of what was and what was not. She should have felt the fullness of the experience in its totality. However, she acknowledged a strange and perplexing vulnerability during that time.

Her parents were loving—she chose them for this reason—but she sensed in them a certain resistance to welcoming her, as though wanting her to be something other than what she had chosen to be. Their desire to have a child was strong, but, Guìa learned much later, they had wished for a boy. Young Guìa felt the strength of this intention.

Human beings forget that every thought, every intention, every desire is inscribed immediately in the Akashic Annals, an etheric cosmic memory which records and creates all the events of the world. Beings are not aware of the materiality of their hopes and needs and, therefore, often create counter- intention to their wishes.

Guìa falls silent, letting me draw my own conclusions.

I understand that not yet being in the space of survival, she did not have the option at that time to resist anything, especially not her parents' intention: she could only make her parents right by agreeing with them that she was not what she should be, she was not what was expected. Only love was available to her, and she could do no other than concur.

As I think of her still in the transition space between the two worlds, a temporary boudoir, I imagine her being all love, devoid of judgments and protection, while in the dawning of human feelings. And I understand that her first emotion, almost human but not quite yet, had been to be sad not to fulfill her parents' wishes. The feeling of not being the one they expected desolated her, a kind of deflation that came from the supreme humility of pure consciousness. She was not what they hoped for. Guìa thus experienced the first imbalance between divine intention and material reality.

She smiles and stands up, indicating that our day is over. I instinctively go to her side, and she leans on me tenderly. Without a word, I accompany her toward the door of her house, and leaving me at the threshold, she goes inside and shuts it gently, without any noise

Walking back toward the village, I think about how quickly my life moved away from the mundane. From Paris to the wild coast of Africa, from conventional thinking to mystical inquiry, I have come a long way. I now wear African dresses better suited to the climate of the place, and my hair is not styled, giving me a wilder, more natural look. I am tanned, walking everywhere in my locally made cord sandals, and bathing anywhere I find water. It is not unusual for insects and animals to let me approach them; they sometimes even come toward me. Trees and flowers are my companions. I am content. I am in the right place at the right time.

PART II

THE CONTEXT
OF THE EGO

CHAPTER 3

THE TIME OF INFANCY

I go to Guìa's house the next morning at dawn, apprehensive and impatient at the same time. The sun is rising on a tranquil sea, and somehow its calm comforts me. Her stories, or perhaps I should say her lessons, have churned my reality and penetrated to the depths of my Self. I have taken in her words like a pupil in front of a master, discovering for the first time the delight of thinking instead of having thoughts. The abyss opening before me requires that I rush into it without reason or certainty. This frightens me at times.

I sit on the sand, waiting for her to appear, my mind gliding gently through the memories of my childhood. I cannot remember much, but some images drift back: a time when I played with my brother; pets I rescued from the street and tried to hide in our garage, so my parents would not give them away; the feel of a white bunny toy that I cuddled when I needed comfort. I remember the birthday when I did not get the paint box I so desired, and the time when a friend broke my kite. But I cannot make sense of it all, nor find an existential meaning to what seems a very normal life.

Guìa appears a few hours later. I join her in the now familiar chairs on the veranda, ready to listen to her sharing.

She tells me she was born in Algeria in the years when war was tearing that country apart. Yet life there, she says, was still delicious and magical. The smells were exotic and spicy. The colors burst with sunshine. The city swirled with an array of styles of dress, more or less modest, representing the entire range of feminine and masculine. The men were swarthy and virile, and spoke loudly. Everything was rocked by a mellow wind brought by the sea, which should have placated this world.

Guìa's parents lived on a farm a few hours' travel from town. Supported by an army of servants, they raised five children. Their family was a close unit. One grandfather was an adventurer who had traveled the world, from Japan to Africa, equipped with the stylish automobiles and Winchester rifles of days gone by. He kept hard-earned hunting trophies as evidence of his masculinity, balanced by a collection of Japanese prints, daring in their subject matter. Guìa describes one grandmother as pure and hard, one of many pioneering women who could work several agricultural properties by herself and bear a dozen children, each wilder than the last. Brothers and sisters, relations by marriage, cousins and friends—all formed a diverse group, a sort of microcosm of the world.

The bravery of these settlers would startle us now, she tells me, but bravery has been an accepted part of human heritage since the beginning of time.

Resilience always surprises observers, although it is obvious that ordinary, everyday life takes hold of its rhythm without exception, at all times and in spite of all events. Normality always wins its place, even in the face of danger. In defiance of the war, the natives and settlers, rich and poor, continued to live their lives. loving each other, arguing with passion, and offering support when tragedy struck. Trouble brought them even closer and forged indestructible bonds.

Only the renegades resisted and suffered, their thirst for freedom incomprehensible to others at a time when invasion and tyranny were facts of life. These were also the rebels who wanted to change lives and reshape the status quo, even at the cost of destroying all things.

I never heard judgment in Guìa's voice, and she offers no opinions as she speaks. For her, there is neither good nor evil, truth nor deceit, praise nor blame. There are only human beings struggling with the irresistible urge to be right. Guìa tells me that her mother, twenty years old at the time, walked her children with a small gun hidden under the cover of the stroller—a futile gesture in the face of yawning danger. She describes her not as a fool, but as a young mother and wife full of tenderness and joy, who thought her love was nearly enough to shield her family from attack.

Guìa describes herself as an infant, her bottomless gaze filled with the intelligence of the soul and the power of divine energy that women have always recognized in the little ones.

The intelligence of the soul is stronger than the pragmatic intelligence needed to survive earthly life. Do not forget that the path to yourself goes through liberation from identification with any experience.

I do not understand. I raise an eyebrow or somehow give her the impression I am missing what she is trying to teach me, because she then provides an example, drawn from her life. I come to realize it as her plunge into the ego of her survival, the moment when she forgot her divinity and eternal nature for a very long time.

One evening, her parents' farm was attacked by men with machine guns. Two-year-old Guìa lay in her mother's arms when the window of the room shattered under gunfire. The curtains flew. Frightened beyond belief, her mother, in an understandable reflex—Guìa emphasizes this fact—threw her child onto the bed before running for Guìa's father, who had weapons of defense on hand.

Imagine this little girl who was heaved onto the bed. What did she feel?

Little Guìa felt betrayed. The original pact between child and protective mother was broken as she was left, helpless, in the face of danger. In her world, her mother had thrown her to her death. She was not only terrified, but furious.

This is the precise moment of my fall from grace. The moment I told myself my mother was throwing me to my death, my interpretation became my truth, and I never questioned its validity. I propelled myself into the deceptive world of survival, where I was not aware of the difference between what was happening and my interpretation of it. I entered the world of unconsciousness.

My interpretations could have stopped right there, perhaps leaving my relationship with my mother bruised but manageable. Instead, caught in the vortex of illusion, I likened one specific incident to the whole of life. In other words, "My mother threw me to my death" became "Life is a place where people throw me to my death." When I gave that meaning to life, it colored my view of everything that was happening at the time and would happen in the future. The trap was set for me to construct my ego, and I forgot everything else.

I am stunned. Can it be so simple? Can a moment of stress, or terror, in Guìa's case, really trigger the loss of our divinity? I can now understand better what she told me yesterday about survival being a reaction to danger. But nothing so dramatic happened to me as a child, and it is difficult to imagine that I lived through a similar moment.

I keep listening, trying to let my memories of such a time arise in my mind.

The episode itself is not important—it is what we do with it. Shall we let it go? Or shall we equate a single incident with the whole of life? To find your "forgetting" moment, you must look at your life and the emotions that repeat themselves over and over again. You may notice one or two major ones. I experienced terror and rage all my life, even when the circumstances did not warrant such a reaction. I wondered for a long time why those feelings persisted. It was only when I remembered it all that I understood the infernal, vicious circle of surviving. Fear and anger flooded my being during the machine gun incident. If you can identify incongruous, recurring emotions and remember the first time you experienced them, you will recall your fall into survival.

A light shines on what she is trying to tell me. During the chaos of the armed attack, young Guìa could not separate that specific incident from life as a whole. Mortal danger brought on by her mother's reaction *was* life, a view that became a certainty. From that moment on, life appeared to Guìa as a country at war, and it was only logical for her to want to survive this threat.

Having assigned a meaning to life, it became obvious to me that I had to find a solution to surviving what was now a continual attack. My solution was to never rely on anyone and to make sure to get by on my own. I decided: "I will not die; I will survive alone." This decision acted as an existential command and became my motto.

I see this as she speaks it. She is telling me that life is a theater, with a stage and an audience, and our survival is the play that we produce. She is saying that, early in our lives, we write what will become a tragedy, a comedy, a poem, a dance, or any other work of art that might result from our decision.

Her life was scripted from that fateful moment on. Her play, she tells me, turned out to be a heroic tragedy. The sets were designed and erected during various developments in her life. The cast came and went, according to circumstances. It seemed a noble pursuit of truth, but it was not the whole story, as Shakespeare profoundly expresses in *Macbeth*: "Life is a tale told by an idiot, full of sound and fury, signifying nothing." So, Guìa walked through life, stubbornly playing the part she had created for herself. Had she never come to understand the illusion of this role, it would have simply defined her story until the time of her death.

> *If you're feeling sorry for the girl, or if you doubt my experience, you are missing what is important: that from the moment I gave a meaning to life, I was no longer in reality but in my story. Life is not and will never be a place where the purpose of people is to betray me! Eight billion people do not wake up every morning thinking of ways to throw me to my death! That is only one meaning given to life by a little girl in a moment of fear. That's the play.*

She adds a detail that seems important to her.

> *My decision was not a conscious one, because had I been conscious, I would have resisted the lure of survival; neither was it unconscious, though, because that would mean I was not present. I call it a moment of perception without awareness, or a moment of unconscious perception, which includes feelings and thoughts, but not choice.*

I can grasp this by holding it up alongside my life. If my history were a play, it would be a romantic musical. I have often been able to sing my way out of difficulties, charming others to obtain what I desire, dancing away my stress, or skipping through my duties. When this does not work—when success eludes me like a jilting lover—my main recurring emotions are hurt and sadness.

There is a definite pattern to my life, and I start to wonder—slowly at first, and then rushing headlong—if my mindset has determined my experience of the moment. Has my perception prescribed my actions, my thoughts, my attitudes, my relationships—even events themselves? Was all this determined by a child's interpretation, an attempt to make sense of something that happened when I was young? *Is any of it real?*

Guìa does not board the train of my thoughts; she leaves me by myself. As I walk home that night, I turn over in my mind all she has said. The child she had been made no distinction between her view of life and life; she did not see any difference between what had happened and her interpretation of what had happened. This seems typical. A small child looking in the mirror does not ask, "Is that my perspective, or is it reality?" And like a thunderclap waking the world, this thought lifts a previously unseen veil of my personal unconsciousness.

When I was very small, perhaps between the ages of one and two, my father and I were playing on the beach, and he took me to the top of a sand dune. We were going to roll downhill side by side, but for some unknown reason, he let me go alone. I arrived at the bottom of the hill, dizzy, not immediately knowing where he was. The sensations were so sharp that, then and there, I decided life was a place where people abandoned me. And, yes, as I think this now, sadness and hurt wash over me.

What Guìa has told me fits perfectly: since that day, I have been only and always living a point of view rather than a life based in reality.

Stupefaction drives me to my knees. Like a supplicant imploring pardon for her wanderings, I raise my arms toward who knows what, in gratitude for the grace of this moment, the visceral certainty of the illusion of it all. The simple truth is, people do not abandon me; my father simply failed to roll down a sand dune by my side!

I now realize I have never seen the world and life in all their splendor; I have never really seen the people around me. I have only glimpsed a pale picture of these things, distorted by my limited point of view. For the first time, I see the beauty that surrounds me. Life is a magic treasure trove of possibilities. The malleability of my existence depends only on myself.

CHAPTER 4

THE TIME OF CHILDHOOD

The next day, on my journey to Guìa's little house, I observe the plants, the insects, the clouds, and everything around me with new eyes. Every little thing brings me boundless wonder. I do not recognize my surroundings. I move through a magical place where universal laws supersede human laws. For the first time in my life, I acknowledge the exceptional nature of the moment.

Eager to hear Guìa's message today, I give thanks for my good fortune. She greets me with her usual delicious smile. Impatient to begin, she refuses with a casual gesture the sweets I have brought.

> *Once my view of life and the solution to survive it were in place, I needed to fashion some armor to help me confidently navigate the danger life now represented. I saw this protective shell as my personality, or my character. In fact, it is a virtual cage.*

This seems logical to me. Where does our personality come from anyhow? Nobody has ever found in our DNA the gene for humor or intelligence, kindness or perfectionism! I must appear distracted, because Guìa recaptures my attention by leaning forward to catch my gaze.

> *Note that the decision I made did not qualify me in any way. It had to do with the universe from which I was now separate. In other words, I was flawless, like all souls are, in a now dangerous world. My view of life limited me, but much was still possible because there was no separation between me and my Self. That shift occurred, however, as I moved further through childhood.*

This tells me that the life of children up to the age of four, five, or six is a pretty wonderful time. Their uninhibited gales of laughter illustrate their freedom to be. Certainly, there can be difficult or painful moments, but minus personal interpretations, they are fleeting and have no effect on the future.

> *All of this changed for me, abruptly and inexorably, at the age of six, triggered by a simple and automatic thought I had that questioned the order of things. I refused to accept an incident, and I decided that what happened should not have happened. I decided it was wrong. This was my first refusal of what is. I did not examine or challenge the incongruity of my decision, nor did I question myself. In a way, that thought entrapped me.*

She adds that it was a crucial moment in her development. It was the beginning of what was to become a habit of refusing what is and wanting what is not.

We are the only species on this Earth that resists what is. You've never heard a dog complain about having only three legs, right? No, the dog runs as fast as he can to catch up with the others, but never thinks it is unfair or that everything should be different!

She laughs at my perplexity, and I laugh at her laughing.

At that age, I was the universe. Once I responded to the incident with the thought that it should not have happened, though, I shattered that oneness. I wrongly deduced that what had happened was directly related to a flaw in me—a fault, something lacking.

Her logic is perfect. Guìa, the child, perceived herself as the center of the universe. In the next moment, she noticed something wrong in this universe. Therefore, she took it personally; if she had been conscious, she would not have decided that she was imperfect.

I begin to grasp what she wants to teach me. The moment she is talking about landed on the child like a bombshell. She moved from a future where everything was possible to a compromised and limited one because of her own perceived defects and imperfections.

For the first time in my life, I experienced a separation from myself, a duality. I saw myself as a person. I used the word "I" to describe myself. This was the beginning of myself as an individual. I gave meaning to the incident, and this meaning was a judgment on my own worth. I was not perfect anymore; I was missing something.

And she tells me what happened.

One day when Guìa was six years old, her mother took her in her arms, gave her a huge hug, and said, "Darling, my darling, I love you so much. And to think that when you were born, I wanted a boy!"

The hug was very good, the declaration of love even more so. But the only thing Guìa retained from the interaction was that her mother had wanted a boy. At that point, the experience of being perfect left her forever. She decided she had a flaw, enormous and irreparable: she was not a boy.

Guìa laughs when she tells me about this incident, but I begin to sour on the pain engendered by what she calls a game. How can she talk about it so lightly? The sadness created by all these misunderstandings makes me resist the absurdity of the ego. The more I resist, the more I plunge into survival, and the more she laughs at me.

But then I remember that sadness is the emotion associated with *my* ego. And at that moment, I can listen openly again.

She continues.

> I drew many things from this pronouncement: I am not wanted, I am not as good as a boy, I am inferior, and all kinds of other interpretations. In the minutes or hours following that decisive moment, I had to find a way to compensate for my flaw. According to my logic, in order to survive the rest of my life without being a boy, I had to try to be as strong as a boy! Therefore, I had to be a superwoman.

From that point on, Guìa decided that she would compete with the boys, to prove, at all costs, she was as strong as they were. She sought not to diminish them, but to be accepted as their equal.

She dove into the most physically masculine disciplines, attempting to master them, from horseback riding, swimming, and water skiing as a child, to piloting helicopters, skydiving, and hang-gliding, as an adult. She once crossed the Pacific Ocean on a boat without autopilot or radio, as if to show herself as daring as any man. But this did not change her reality. As she speaks, she bursts out laughing at the absurdity of the trap in which she put herself: no matter how hard she tried to be a boy, she never became one!

> *Becoming a helicopter pilot is fine. But in doing so, the admiration I inspired was for the woman who had accomplished it. This only reinforced my failure at being a boy! And striving to be as good as a male did me no favors in my relationships with men.*

Of course, it didn't. Lacking confidence in the woman she was, Guìa spent her time trying to impress others. This only made her appear arrogant, contrary to her desired effect. Men rejected her, turned off by what they thought was aloofness and snobbery.

I am touched by Guìa's authenticity as she describes all of this. Imparting what she has learned is even more important than the personal insights she gained. She is convinced that a new human culture is possible, a culture in which there is no desire to dominate and win over other people, no drive to "make it," no effort to change others. And she helps me define what had made me so uncomfortable with my argumentative friends back in France. Tinkering with making people better was not the goal; simply existing for each other was.

> *I had a huge problem, do you understand? I had to survive the rest of my life with what I now thought was an irreparable flaw in me. To do so, I had to hide this fault; I could not afford to show this weakness. The only option I had was to compensate for this disability. I had to live contrary to the truth, as I have told it to you, which is that everything is possible in our lives.*

I grasp the absurdity of the trap in which she imprisoned herself. I listen carefully to what follows.

> *The notion of compensation is paramount in the survival mechanism, because understanding it is the secret of getting out of the trap. For instance, to arrive at equilibrium, a scale with a weight of x pounds on the left-hand platter needs the same weight on the right-hand platter. To apply this analogy to myself, on the left-hand platter was my flaw—I was not a boy—and on the right-hand platter was my compensation— being a superwoman. My survival depended on the perfect equilibrium of the scale. I could never allow one of the trays to empty itself, thus creating my trap. The more I demonstrated that I was a superwoman, the more I felt the impossibility of being a boy. I could never reach satisfaction!*

She pauses for emphasis.

The link between the decision and the compensation for the decision needs to be broken. Only then will you be liberated by realizing the illusion of it all: you cannot fix what is not broken.

What Guìa shares forces me to question my desire for perfection. Does this not cause me much suffering? I realize that I have constantly lived with the fear of being incapable in the back of my mind, and listening to Guìa, I finally question the validity of this fear. I realize that compensating for this fear by trying to be perfect has been my own way of surviving.

Yet, the more I sought perfection, the more I reinforced the experience of being incapable. In trying to achieve perfection, I have had to limit risk-taking, which only made me feel incapable all over again. I now understand the lack of success and passion in the life I left. Taking my reasoning one step further, it dawns on me that the risk I took by hastily leaving that life behind is what finally led me to fulfill my dream of adventure. Thus, I found a way out of the vicious cycle of my arbitrary decisions.

I do not know how Guìa is following my thoughts, but she picks up where they leave off.

These survival mechanisms are not bad, but they limit everyone and exclude the possible. Compensation is one of the sources of the lack of ontological freedom. It produces the desired result, to survive, but it is inseparable from the defect for which it is compensating. Contentment is not possible in this system.

I grasp the mechanism. The illusion of being defective is the defense mechanism of a child under stress. The compensation can never suffice, since the flaw is itself an invention of the child. The absurdity of survival lies in trying to fix something that is not broken in the first place. I see my own role in this misbegotten quest as similar to a dog chasing its tail: the dog will never succeed in catching it, but what enthusiasm, what stubbornness!

I start to laugh. Since I was very, very young, I have been completely inauthentic, thinking I am defective and spending a lifetime hiding it. I have only shown the world my compensation, not my Self. When I was a child, my parents and my grandparents lauded my desire for perfection. But the child I was, and the adult I became, had no innate personality. I had only a strategy.

Guìa validates my thinking.

> *Nobody has ever seen a baby in a cradle and raved about its character or personality. Babies certainly have a recognizable quality or essence, but the limits imposed by a personality are absent. Their character arises only later, as a result of the compensation that is put in place to try to repair the faults they see in themselves.*

And she anticipates my question.

> *You're going to ask me how to get out of the trap. But the real trap is the attempt to get out of the trap. Because the trap is not real! There is no need to look for a way out. There is nothing to*

do other than to become aware of it.

Then she gives me an analogy to help me understand this idea.

> *It is very simple to capture a monkey. Start by putting a big bunch of bananas in a transparent container with a narrow opening. The monkey will be attracted by the smell and put its arm into the container to grab the bananas, but will be unable to pull the them back through the small opening. The hunter can then approach and capture the monkey, because it does not want to let go of the bananas. All the animal has to do to be free is to open its hand. But in clinging to the bunch of bananas, the monkey loses its freedom.*

My mouth falls open at the clarity of this example. Guìa believes people are in the same predicament as the monkey in her story. We hold on to opinions, evaluations, decisions we make. We inauthentically pretend we cannot let go. She expresses this without judgment, and with great compassion. For her, the condition of the world is inauthenticity, and it is a symptom, not a fatal disease.

It was not easy, she admits, to arrive at a level of consciousness where she could be aware of actually having decided to be a superwoman, because it seemed so inherent. Once she took responsibility for that decision, she acquired a great deal of freedom. She was still able to reap the benefits of the superwoman she had become without the weight of the sentence she had passed on herself.

Old age can be a difficult time if you do not do the work of taking responsibility for the trap in which you have locked yourself throughout your life. After a while, your compensation mechanisms will no longer work, and only the illusory decisions you made about your faults will remain. You will then suffer even more.

For Guìa, letting go was as simple as opening her hand and releasing the bunch of bananas that had cost her her freedom. Simple, but not easy, she adds. But doing this was necessary for her to reach the place of peace and well-being she was committed to attaining.

Night is falling, and I slip away, lost in my thoughts once again. The dust of the trail has settled, the night noises of the wilderness surrounding me are rising—strange animals calling to each other, leaves in the bushes suddenly shake—but I do not react. I am too bewildered by what I am discovering inside. If the survival mechanisms Guìa has described ensnare everyone in the world, are we all condemned to this human trap forever?

CHAPTER 5

THE TIME BETWEEN CHILDHOOD
AND ADOLESCENCE

The next day, Guìa reminisces. To illustrate her mode of surviving, she tells me about her life as a little girl.

She tells me she had a quick and agile mind, and was very capable   at school. She smiles at my visible admiration, finding it funny that   I venerate something that, for her, was only a consequence of having decided to be a superwoman. And as I doubt that her intelligence was merely a function of her decision, she illustrates the trap of the ego by relating a key moment of her childhood.

> *I always finished my classwork well before the others, so my teacher played with me to keep me occupied while we waited. I adored him. I think he liked my vivacious spirit and my love of challenges. One day, he didn't have time to entertain me, and I found myself with nothing to do. As I looked around the classroom, I noticed for the first time that the other students were nibbling at their fingers and holding their heads, seeming to struggle to finish the exercise I had completed a good fifteen minutes earlier. A weight fell on my shoulders. My greatest*

anxiety was that I would not be wanted, and here, I was too different. I was afraid the other students would reject me. The superwoman was not going to work in this case. So, I decided to hide my intellectual ability and stop shining.

From that day until the end of her schooling, Guìa never did a homework assignment and never listened to a lesson. Because of her intelligence, she was still able to earn average marks, and this suited her, because she didn't want to shine.

When our compensation does not work anymore, our only recourse is to destroy what is possible. This is another way to survive. In my logic of survival, I had to vanquish what I perceived as a new threat—being smarter than the others. But there was another side to this choice that I did not see: the price I would pay for resorting to this destructive mechanism.

Guìa didn't apply herself to her studies for a long time, and she came to believe she was stupid, or at least not very intelligent. The circumstances of her life flowed from this belief. By dint of not working and aiming to be only average, she would sometimes fail, throwing her back into the usual panic of not being as good as the boys.

It is a fundamental truth that, in this life, we always reap what we sow. I planted the seeds of my flawed nature, my lack of intelligence, and what I harvested was a belief that these things were true. This belief affected my actions from then on.

I understand the illusion of the reality she created for herself, but I am still unclear on how.

> *My only tool for creating is language. When I talk about language, I'm talking about my thoughts as well as my spoken words. I have many options to make sense of or talk about the world: language can be symbolic, such as mathematics; descriptive, evocative such as poetry; technical or creative. Most of us take language for granted, very much like the air we breathe. I, for one, certainly never questioned my use of language, nor its eventual role in my life.*

Like a rocket headed for a target, I realize the depth of power we possess, as she points out that it was through language that she created that illusion. Until this moment, I have never considered that language is the source of our reality. Once again, she helps me discover a new realm of possibility. I reflect on the role language plays in each profession. Doctors, lawyers, philosophers, artists, and scientists have each mastered a specific language. Without this lexicon, they cannot possibly master the world in which they have chosen to operate.

If I ever find myself on an operating table and, through the lull of anesthesia, hear the surgeon say, "Nurse, give me the little cutting instrument over there," this lack of specificity will be a clear indication of the doctor's incompetence. I will get up immediately, sleepy or not, and run away! The small cutting instrument is called a scalpel, and if the surgeon doesn't know that term, I will have to presume I am dealing with a quack.

I can see that language is not simply crucially descriptive but also has a creative function. A ring can be just a ring, or it can be an engagement ring, creating a new reality of two people ready to commit to a life together. A house can be just that, but it can also be a home to a family or a shelter to homeless people. An animal can be a pet. By contrast, numbers are not to be found in reality. I can point at a tree, but I cannot point at a number. I am realizing that there are, indeed, two different languages.

Guìa goes on.

> *I can describe the world, explain situations, and talk about events I've experienced. This use of language is practical but will not impact the very things I speak about. The language of description is, therefore, the language of the spectator, in that it has no influence on the game. I can criticize, judge, or encourage, but I cannot actually play the game. I can be safe sitting in the stands, but I will not know the vitality of being a player, taking risks on the field, being in the action. I will not win, nor will I lose.*

> *There is another language which creates my being and, so, my reality. Something is born in the precise moment of speaking that did not exist previously, and the rest of my life is altered forever, because that articulation influenced the future.*

> *The day of our wedding ceremony, at the very moment the priest declares us married, our life alters. We become married "until death do us part." This language creates a new life, a new future, a new experience of being alive. The transformative*

language of creation is called a declaration.

I am able to see that the language of declaration is independent of any past event, of any interpretation or circumstance. If I say, "I have been abandoned," this is what I will get, with its plethora of emotions and feelings. If I say my father did not roll down the hill with me, ditto.

The repercussions of being careless with language put me in awe of my power: If I use swear words, if I do not honor what I say, if I break my promises, I will create chaos in my life. I make a promise to myself that, from this point on, I will cherish language for what it is: my tool to create my reality. My power. I have a say in the matter of what I create.

After I take my leave of Guìa for the evening, I am so fascinated by what I have discovered that I continue to walk beyond the village without even noticing it. The night is falling, but I am in another space; I have discovered my power to create my life. I wonder to myself which decisions I have made without being aware of this ability, decisions that have no doubt dominated and imprisoned me.

I long for the night to end so I can ask Guìa to confirm my thoughts. Upon my return in the early morning, she does, offering her congratulations.

You now understand that language can create, which leads to action, and then to the results that follow. It always starts with language. If I use descriptive words, which by definition describe something that is already present, I am subject to the past and limited. If I create from nothing, then everything is possible. And we must also remember that language is equivocal, since different people attribute different meanings to words.

I feel she has a lot more to add, but, perhaps, she knows exactly what my intake limits are. In the few days since I met her, a revolution has taken place in my previously ordained world. I think she knows how to dose her teachings so as not to frighten me. She tells me anecdotes all morning, and she is right to do so. I relax, little by little.

She tells me of the day when she was ten years old and had to have an intimate examination by a male doctor because he thought she had appendicitis. This man must have been a fool, with no sensitivity for a girl of that age. Her mother held her hand and explained that women have to endure this kind of personal intrusion. This strengthened Guìa's conviction that being a woman was not a gift.

She tells me that her friends in school were always boys, and that girls did not like her because of it. She also tells me about games and other things that brought her joy, the beauty of the life her family provided, and the security that came from never questioning the love they freely gave. She says it is thanks to this love that she can describe her childhood as happy.

During this time, she was afraid at night because a black witch came to visit her. She hid under the sheets, paralyzed with fear that if she moved, she would be in danger. She tells me her mother covered her with a silk scarf at bedtime, saying it would protect her from all danger. She describes to me how this scarf, carrying the delicious scent of her mother, allowed her to sleep well. The simplicity and abundance of the life offered by her parents gave her some stability, which allowed her to cope with life.

I think of all the other children who live through the same thing, in their own way, of course, and struggle to hide their fear, their anguish, and their worries. I understand why Guìa wants so much for me to write her story. She is all love and wants only to relieve the suffering of others.

CHAPTER 6

THE TIME OF ADOLESCENCE

It rains the next day, a very rare thing. The palms of the coconut trees shelter us from the warm, welcome drops. Seated before Guìa, I still do not ask questions, because I want to hear what she finds important. As usual, she begins to speak, assuming that I am listening. And she is right. I drink in her words.

> *Soon after I condemned myself as damaged, I reached the age of eleven or twelve. My communities became important, now that I had enough presence of mind to expand my attention from myself to others. I became aware of my close environment: my friends, my siblings, my family.*

Since Guìa's main concern was to belong to those groups and communities, as it is all of our focus at that age, she matched her actions to those of others. She tried speaking like everyone else, wearing the same kind of clothing as her friends. She also wanted her parents to be like those of her peers. She blended in and identified with her groups. She belonged, as a given.

Guìa was also growing up, and she had become passionate about riding horses. In the small village in which she lived, there was a riding club at the end of an alley lined with pink laurel bushes. She went there every day. This particular club hosted only stallions, so as to avoid any natural breeding frenzy. The stallions fought with each other and were often hard to manage, but Guìa was a very skilled rider. So, even though she did not own a horse, she was trusted and always got to ride the best horses.

Her favorite mount was a tall and strong Anglo-Arab stallion with a shiny chestnut coat. He belonged to the national army but was at the riding club to be trained. The girl formed a close bond with this horse. In her mind and heart, he was hers, her friend, her companion.

> One day, after much insistence on a friend's part, I allowed her to ride "my" horse. Unfortunately, she could not control him. They got too close to another stallion, which then kicked my horse. My friend was thrown, and the two steeds fought, and ultimately, my horse's leg was broken.
>
> It is very difficult to save a horse with a broken leg. They tied him up and tried to make him lie down, his damaged limb dangling. There was blood everywhere, and my horse was neighing in pain. The adults finally fetched a gun, and to my utmost despair, they shot my horse in the temple. I think they forgot I was there, a powerless witness to this humane tragedy.

I can easily imagine a young girl of eleven in this situation, forgotten by all the adults. Guìa ran home as fast as she could, sobbing, only wanting her parents to comfort her and take away the burden of this experience. She made it to her parents' bedroom and found her mother.

My mother saw what must have been a very desperate look on my face, and she was suddenly overwhelmed by terror, thinking one of my siblings was dead or injured.

Trying to catch her breath so she could speak, Guìa immediately said it was her horse that had been killed. Her mother, in understandable shock, reproached Guìa for frightening her, calling her irresponsible and dramatic.

Listen carefully to how the ego works. Do not be distracted by the drama of the story. Listen to what matters, which is the decision I made in the face of my mother's reaction to my distress. Seeing the terror I caused her, I decided I was a selfish monster. How could I be so self-centered and think only of myself and my troubles? I compared myself to my siblings and was certain they would never have scared our mother in this way.

Listen and understand: the survival mechanism of the ego further took over my life in that moment. I decided I was different from my siblings. They were nice, and I was a monster with unacceptable emotions and feelings. I had to change if I wanted to be accepted by my family. I had to hide my anguish and my fears. I had to be brave and swallow my pain.

Guìa decided to hide her pain and say nothing of what happened that day, so as not to frighten the people she loved. Her parents would not know the horror she lived through until much, much later, once she became an adult.

This further illustrated to me the trap of the ego: understanding our strength is also, and always, our weakness. Guìa became courageous and brave to hide her fear of being a monster, but the price she paid (before she realized the absurdity of her decisions) was to experience a life of loneliness, without any support—because she made sure no one ever knew about her suffering. This decision prevented her from entrusting her pain to anyone, and this was a heavy burden to carry throughout her life.

> *To survive means to exist despite adversity. The illusion of having to repair what was broken in myself was deep because I firmly believed I was flawed. It is this very illusion that is a trap and is the source of suffering.*

Guìa offers me access to freedom, like a set of keys. She uses her most intimate memories to convey her message about the illusion of suffering. And yet, this does not elevate her. She regards her life as ordinary, useful, no more than an illustration of the trap of the ego.

That evening, walking by the sea on the way back to the village, I glimpse the meaning I have given to my life as perhaps a story invented by none other than myself. I catch a whiff of the extent of my need for identification, as if I always have to come up with an explanation for everything, as if I have to fill a void I cannot tolerate. I can be free of that. Once I arrive at the village, I watch the sunset without any identification, completely present in a moment of deep, existential calm. The villagers understand my need for silence, and the gathering around the fire that evening becomes a collective meditation.

CHAPTER 7

THE TIME OF ADULTHOOD

The sun rises again, and with it my doubts. Everything Guìa has taught me suddenly seems far too simplistic: the pain I have felt and still feel, the emotion, the fears—they are not an illusion. Children dying of hunger, war—they are not an illusion. How dare Guìa reduce everything to choice, to interpretation?

Reluctantly, I make my way back to her house, my arguments formed. She gives me a sad smile as I forget them. The more I argue, the more insubstantial her body seems to become, almost fading away, as if it might disappear altogether. For a time—how strange this must sound—I wonder if she is even human.

My regression causes her to lump me in with my past and those problematic friends of mine.

> *Your refusal to accept the simplicity of the system of survival is the reason nothing has changed since the beginning of time. You identify yourselves with your stories and what is observable: your body, your personality, your character, your thoughts,*

your emotions, and the circumstances of the world. Stifled by an undifferentiated ego, you lack consciousness.

The same patterns are repeated century after century. On the one hand, we now have more technological means, and our living conditions are continually improving; but on the other, we are always destroying ourselves. Humankind does not transform itself, which leaves a destructive expansion of technology as our only option: the only progress we make is in our capacity to destroy ourselves.

I do not have an answer, because the enormity of the violence and suffering that has taken place throughout our history speaks for itself. We remain silent for a long moment. She gives me the time I need to accept for myself the veracity of her remarks.

After deciding how to survive by myself and how to survive in groups, I then put the last part of my personality in place when I was faced with the problem of having to survive the circumstances of life. The story I will tell you is of the event that determined the beginning of my adulthood, when, for the third time, I interpreted an event as proof of my inadequacy. One of my greatest existential fears was that I would be left alone to deal with the circumstances of life. This event confirmed that I was, indeed, alone.

She tells me what happened.

She went to a convent school, a protective environment where sports and knowledge predominated. Physical love was not something she encountered there. Certainly, she had loved a boy in her childhood, but her passion extended no further than sitting next to him on the school bus. She had been educated about sex by her mother, who, as modernity obliged, told her about physical passion. Guìa was not expected to wait until marriage to make love, but she was advised to choose with care the man to whom she would give her virginity. Because her mother presented it as such, Guìa saw physical love as wonderful and divine. She waited patiently to taste this gift of life, as a gourmet anticipates a dessert, knowing that the waiting is part of the delectation itself.

Teenaged Guìa looked older than her years, but the nature of her upbringing had protected her from many aspects of adult life, including the advances of men. When she was seventeen, her parents gave permission for her to stay for a visit with one of their friends. This woman, whom Guìa loved deeply, did not have children and could not imagine the innocence of the young girl. This friend lent Guìa clothes and allowed her to wear makeup, a first for Guìa, who was delighted.

One evening, they went to dinner with a forty-year-old man, who pointedly flirted with Guìa. She discovered the thrill of being courted as a woman, and she confesses to me that she flirted with this man in return.

At some point after dinner, he proposed they go to a nightclub. Guìa's elder friend did not want to join them, but she encouraged Guìa to go along without her. Unsettled by this unfamiliar scenario, Guìa's inexperience and shyness stopped her from declining the invitation. She found herself alone in this man's car, silent and incapacitated by the anguish of not knowing how to handle the new situation.

The man drove to his home under the pretext of having to put on a tie, and once in front of his building, he asked her to come up to his apartment with him, saying it was too dangerous for her to stay alone in the car.

> *You understand, I did not know how to decline. I was paralyzed by the fear of not knowing what to say to him, but I never imagined he would rape me. Such a thing was not in my reality. I loved my father, my hero, and my experience of men was based on my relationship with him. I had an image of men as protective and honorable. I had never met a predator.*
>
> *I said nothing as he violated me; I did not fight. When he hurt me and I screamed, he harshly told me to be quiet, and I obeyed. I dissociated from it all, oblivious from then on to the experience of trauma.*

She has never been able to remember what happened immediately after this event. All she knows is that she woke from a kind of trance to find herself in the shower, in her friend's apartment, in shock, washing herself frantically. She felt utterly alone to face the enormity of this circumstance: no one could repair the loss of her virginity and the violence of the action. In her eyes, she had only one option: to make herself wrong for being so naïve, to blame herself for being so stupid, and to find a way to survive yet again.

I am shocked as much by her story as by her calm while recounting it. I can feel her authentic non-attachment from those circumstances. There is a part of her that is beyond my emotional and physical reality. I do not have her degree of non-attachment, and so I suffer in her place.

For a long time, she was angry at the predator who took advantage of her. For years, her view of herself stayed stuck at that young age. She considered herself a wounded person in constant danger, and she was not able to see and experience herself as the adult woman she became. That discrepancy—having become an adult, yet still seeing herself as an adolescent—had consequences. She says the photos taken of her during that time reveal a profound sadness despite her smiles. This sadness, she tells me, came from having had her choice ripped away from her. It persisted until she realized that her body had been affected but had healed, and that her Self was never damaged. Achieving a profound relationship with reality was a liberation.

> *Beyond the outrage and abuse, rape dispossesses the person who suffers it of his or her free will. The predator identifies with his desires, and his need for self-satisfaction makes him unable to face any reality other than his own. Rape can never be justified, because it is based on the desire to control and to use the life of another. This man stole an important moment of my life, and I lost it forever. He took what did not belong to him.*

She smiles and explains gently how she had the strength to overcome this ordeal. I wonder if she, somehow, knows I have experienced a similar trial. Perhaps. We never talk about it, for what she has told me is enough to free me from the demons of my past.

The important thing is not what happened. That is the past, and as I have told you, I survived. The important thing is that I carried for years the burden of the decisions I made because of what happened. I, indeed, decided I was naïve and stupid to have put myself in that situation. I wanted to be sure it would never happen again. I thought my only recourse was to face the circumstances of life alone. To survive my decisions, I compensated by developing a way of being that I would describe as resourceful. It was logical, because I needed to find solutions to make up for my stupidity. That was my ontological survival.

She is determined that I understand what she wants me to learn.

According to the logic of survival, the situation I experienced with this man was terrible and should not be repeated. I locked myself into a trap when I decided to spend the rest of my life trying to avoid an event that would never be repeated, anyway, as I would never be seventeen again.

She became stuck in this identification with the wounded young girl. She was only finally released when she realized, years later, she was not that girl anymore but was, in fact, a full-grown woman. Although she had been attacked by a predator, she had managed to survive, and suddenly, in a flash of realization, she could finally be proud of herself. She had survived a real physical danger, and that was what survival was for, to triumph over a danger of physical death. She was no longer a little abused fawn but a deer in full power of her means. She could recognize the predators and dismiss them. She would never be defenseless again.

Responding to my silence and amazement at what she is telling me, Guìa concludes the day with one of her existential lessons.

> *This is how I forged my personality. Once I fabricated my view of life at the age of two, I decided how I was going to relate to myself at the age of six, to groups at twelve, and finally to life at seventeen. The design of the ego is absolutely brilliant, as each decision corresponds to a stage of our development. The rest of my life would only be a repetition of these incidents I have described to you, until I realized, little by little, that I was responsible for those decisions—that the circumstances of life, however tragic they may be, did not condemn me to being a victim.*

> *Acceptance, darling, is the path to freedom. In the best-case scenario, age and experience lead us to let go and to realize the absurdity of the game of survival. The weakening of our body, the bitterness of failures, the futility of success, the despair of suffering, the disappointed hope of an imagined future, but also the ephemeral nature of happiness and our constant dissatisfaction all lead us to this understanding. In the best case. Otherwise, we realize the absurdity of survival a few minutes before dying, and it is then too late to discover life.*

With a long sigh, she gets up and retires for the day, no doubt exhausted from her long monologue.

After her departure, I spend hours examining my life, trying to make sense of it all. How many times have I sworn to myself to stop being nice, to stop saying yes, to stop trying to please others? Then, in spite of my resolve, I'd done these things anyway, like a machine programmed to continuously produce the same results. I have so often promised myself to tell off those who have tried to take advantage of me, but once face to face with them, I have been incapable of doing so. I have felt sentenced to be quiet and keep my opinions to myself, to hide them behind a fake smile.

I am not alone. I have had friends who promised to stop working so much, to spend more time with their family and their children, but never realized they didn't do it until it was too late. The children grew up, their spouse left them, and they were still working long hours.

I once met someone who was incapable of resisting his need to make jokes, and it embarrassed him. He swore to himself to stop doing it, again and again, to no avail. He continued to employ humor as a shield, especially in inappropriate places, like funerals. The more he tried to control himself, the worse it got.

I realize Guìa is right.

Maybe we are all on autopilot, under the command of the survival mechanisms we have ourselves created, and no matter how much we intend to, we cannot behave contrary to those mechanisms.

The trap of survival is cruel because it functions perfectly. I have survived wonderfully. On the other hand, I have not lived. My mind is agitated as it perceives how the limits created by these mechanisms have prevented me from achieving the exceptional.

I am starting to become aware of how immense a disruption Guìa's sharing of her story is going to be in my life. I can sense it. As I go to my bed, I hope sleep will be my best chance at escape, but it is not to be.

CHAPTER 8

A DREAM

I have a shattering night.

I dream of a little girl with gold curls, who wakes up one evening when her parents come back from the movies. Totally awake and thinking it is morning, she rushes into the living room, laughing, singing, dancing, ready to start a new day. This is not an intention shared by her parents, who are sleepy and want her in bed. They let her know.

The little girl does not understand why they want to spoil a wonderful moment with an incomprehensible rule. She is disappointed and frustrated, helpless. In my dream, I see the little girl decide that life is a place where people prevent her from doing what she wants to do, and that she has no choice in the matter; she has to obey. I shout to her without any sound, like we do in dreams, trying in vain to make her understand that her perception is not true, that she does have a choice. She cannot hear me. I see her luminosity fade and her vital energy darken, but I am a helpless witness.

Then I see her at age five, going on a bicycle adventure alone. After some time, she realizes she is lost. Her father looks everywhere for her, and when he finds her, he appears to her as a savior. But instead of the hug she expects from him, she gets a slap. And again, in my nightmare, I see her decide she is a naughty little girl as she tries to excuse her father's reaction.

Then she is eleven years old, and inadvertently breaks a vase her father gave her mother for their engagement. I see that her mother will not forgive her, and she is severely punished by her father. The girl condemns herself as a bad person and decides she has to become wise and stop doing these stupid things. Her radiance is now almost extinguished, and in my dream, I cannot catch her attention to prevent this.

My nightmare continues as I watch her inexorably lock herself inside a prison she cannot see. Now grown up, political events lead her to leave the country she loves. I see her alone in the face of this loss, but she decides she cannot do anything about it and has to be reasonable. Then, in a terrible moment, I see all of her liveliness disappear, leaving a shell of possibility.

I wake up screaming in pain over the imprisonment of a soul.

This little girl is me. This little girl is us.

PART III

FROM EGO
TO SELF

CHAPTER 9

THE TIME OF LOVE

I wonder the next morning what my meetings with Guìa will now be about, since she told me the rest of her life was only a repetition of what she has already communicated. Does she have anything else to give me?

I have been so profoundly moved by our talks that I do not want them to come to an end. I hope she will be with me for at least a few more weeks. Just in case, I have prepared a list of questions to encourage her to speak, but I don't need it. Guìa wants to tell me about the rest of her life because, she says, smiling, the most important part is her spiritual awakening.

> *I clearly recall that when I was twelve years old, I realized the cocoon in which I lived—a cocoon built by my parents to be soft and secure—was not a reflection of the real world. I knew there was poverty, suffering, misery, and despair, but also beauty, greatness, spirituality, and joy. I felt frustrated at being cut off from its totality. I wanted to communicate my fear of not being able to experience all that is possible on this Earth. I wanted to*

feel and to experiment with the whole of what life had to offer.

I left home at the age of eighteen, in search of adventure. And my life has been exactly what I wanted. I have experienced the greatest happiness and the most profound despair, and eventually I reached the calm of wholeness.

Her first grand experience was love. Guìa was twenty years old and working to pay for her studies when she became the housekeeper for a man called Caelan, who had settled in the European countryside after two failed marriages and four children.

This man, a successful businessman, was intelligent and funny, and older than Guìa's father. He was also unhappy about his failures at love.

His first marriage was a youthful union. The separation, although painful for the mother of his first three children, had only dissolved the link between a man and a woman who had evolved separately over the years, until they no longer shared common interests. The failure of the second marriage, however, had annihilated him.

He had succumbed to the sophisticated and piquant charm of an intelligent and ambitious English woman, who had novel ideas about the sharing and equality of wealth. Their years together were not a success. He was left with the feeling of having been used for his money, without receiving much gratitude or tenderness in return. Eventually, he had a heart attack that almost killed him.

It is always surprising that those who shout the loudest about the need for equality and respect for human rights often despise the people who give them the means to achieve it. Caelan's generosity made it possible for a lot of people to pursue their dreams, including his children and me. He had a gift for making money, and he shared his money with everyone around him.

For the first time, I see Guìa slightly annoyed. The expression is fleeting, though, as is always the case with her emotions. She has already demonstrated her ease with surrendering to all feelings. She never makes emotions wrong. She welcomes them, knowing that wanting to be liberated from them would imply she is held captive, which she never is! She has succeeded at that. No feelings ever constrain her. Everything happening to her is always an integral part of the universe.

Watching her ease with her mental state gives me permission to feel whatever I feel about other people without being frightened, knowing I have the choice not to take chaotic actions based on emotion. She has taught me that feelings are not the guide for what I am doing. Allowing my feelings to just be, and looking upon their coming and going with indifference, gives me peace. What a release it is! One more time, acceptance is the key.

Guìa then tells me how she met and fell in love with this man.

She was twenty, and he was forty-eight. She arrived at night during a snowstorm to a huge house emptied of furniture. Its brown carpeting, navy blue curtains, and yellow walls could not warm the abode, which was as frosty as only the houses of the countryside can be. She found herself face to face with the man and his daughter: two pairs of pale blue eyes, wide and sad, one expressing the bitterness of his failures, the other carrying the weight of her parents' separation. Guìa came from a warm and sunny Mediterranean environment, and this coldness and sadness were unbearable to her.

> *I do not know how I knew what to do, but in only three months, the house was full of laughter and life. We created a weird and mismatched community, but it worked. I was in charge of the school runs, I prepared dinner, organized the gardener and the maid, and then we put the little girl to sleep. Caelan would then pour himself a whiskey and talk to me for hours about life, geography, hope and pain, existentialism and history. In fact, looking back at this time, I now know I tapped into the frequency of a wondrous reality, and as always, I reaped what I sowed. Love is a function of acceptance, and I did just that: Caelan was perfect the way he was, and the way he was not. Our differences were not a separation but were, instead, the glue that gave us our sense of unity, like a fence is a boundary held in common by what is on either side of it.*

I have typically believed that lovers see each other in a most unrealistic light, but in listening to Guìa, I now want to believe it might be possible to see in another the splendor of what a human being really is. Maybe true lovers give each other the real experience of completeness, allowing a new vision of the world.

> *We know the stone is hard because our skin is soft. We experience hardness through the relationship between the hard stone and our soft skin. The sun sends light, but the space around the sun*

will be dark unless there is a planet to reflect it. You cannot give something away unless someone takes it.

For duality to exist, two things must be in relationship with each other, and in that relationship, there is unity. The interrelatedness of the entire universe is reflected in the inseparability of the parts of nature. Human relationship follows the same principle: everything exists as a function of relationship. When that realization happens with a couple, there are no longer two separate people.

For the first few months after their initial meeting, Guìa never thought of Caelan as anything but a mentor. The fact that he was older than her father imposed a respect that precluded any attraction beyond admiration. But she confesses to writing only of him in letters to her parents.

After all, what is love without admiration? Imagine someone patting you on the back saying, "Poor little girl; you're silly, but I like you." Who would want this kind of love?

And she bursts out laughing, describing his average height, his slightly yellow teeth, his balding head, and his feet distorted by a genetic disease that had made it difficult for him to walk. But none of this mattered to her. She had only seen his eyes and delighted in his laugh, listened to the brilliance of his words and felt the depth of his love. She confesses to having had a weakness for his broad shoulders, where she liked to snuggle. He was beautiful to her, a beauty that came from someone with a pure and tender heart.

*One night, after I'd been at his house for four or five months, I
was leaving to go to a party, and he looked at me like a man
looks at a woman who attracts him. I was young and beautiful. I
wore a long, fluid dress, and I had adorned myself like an Indian
princess, with a chain draped across my forehead. Looking me
in the eye, he told me I was wonderful, and I realized just then
that our relationship was going to be turned upside down.*

She blushes a little, probably remembering how she felt in that moment.
I imagine her young, and amorous without knowing it, in a foreign
country, on the cusp of experiencing a love that still transports her to
this day.

She does not tell me about their nights. I think she wants to keep that
chapter of her life as a treasure that belongs to her alone. I like to
imagine that time is her enchanted garden, the place where she likes to
go by herself. I do not intrude as she reminisces; I just watch as she is
silent for a long time until she is ready to speak again.

*Do not think it was a fairy tale right from the beginning. He was
appalled at himself for being with such a young woman. He
blamed himself and wondered if he had become an egocentric
old man who needed to prove his manhood. He kept telling me
not to get attached to him, because he had decided never to be
in love again. He assured me it was no longer possible for him.
We hid our relationship for months, so as not to upset his little
girl. Once the time came, and with the authenticity of a child,
she said only that she thought him too old to have a girlfriend.*

Guìa actually left Caelan's house after a few months of concealing the relationship, telling him that she did not want to live a lie, even though she understood the need for it. If he wanted her to stay, she needed to officially be his girlfriend. In her early wisdom, she preferred to leave with a broken heart rather than spoil what they had. She hoped he would see for himself the strength of her logic. He quickly asked her to return, and she understood this as an acknowledgement of the love he could not yet fully express.

She tells me of her patience with his fears, of how she instilled in him her love for traveling, and of how she gradually tamed him. She speaks of her gratitude for the patience he showed her in return as he calmed her shyness, and how equally grateful she was for the woman she became because of his love.

She tells me of his kindness and concern for his friends and family, and of his love for his children. Once it was clear this relationship was going to last, Guìa was then faced with telling her family that she was in love, and that she was going to live with Caelan. She chokes with laughter as she remembers telling her father over the phone.

> *I asked my father to sit down, and I told him without taking a breath that I was in love with a man who was two years older than he was, who had been married twice, and who had four children!*

I so love her cascading laugh. I think I am witnessing the beauty of the woman in love, the woman made complete by coming together with her other half. I imagine a soul choosing to come to Earth and faced with the need to select a gender, thereby cutting itself off from divine completeness. I understand that the joy she felt came from the meeting of two souls finding universal completeness, like an eternal puzzle. I now understand the concept of the soulmate and discover a new yearning to experience it myself.

Night is falling, and I am afraid Guìa will stop talking. I want to listen to the rest of her story, praying for a happy ending. She does not seem tired and continues.

They tried to have a child. Caelan had had a vasectomy before meeting Guìa, but because of her youth and her deep desire to be a mother, he put aside his concerns about being too old and underwent an operation to reverse it. Guìa admits she confronted him with a difficult choice, and she winks at me.

Me with children—or no children and not with me, I told him.

She relates this with an air of intense satisfaction. He chose her and stopped resisting their age difference.

He called her his Galinnette and told her she must have been an old sage in the Himalayan hills in a previous life. He also whispered to her with benevolent impatience that she was exhausting, with her constant quest for the extraordinary. He held her hand to cross the street, to the great but amused despair of his little girl, who protested at having to witness such a pathetic love story. Caelan built Guìa a huge winter garden with heated flooring, so she could walk barefoot during the wet and frosty winters. He offered her extravagant gifts full of meaning about the celebration of their love.

When Caelan's daughter spent every other month with her mother, the lovers took those opportunities to travel, looking for sun and sea, both passions of Guìa's. They loved this time away from the demands of their everyday life, during which they could feel like they were alone in the world.

> *We chose not to pursue getting married to make sure we did not lose custody of Caelan's daughter, from whose mother Caelan had never legally divorced. I had a deep connection with this smart and courageous girl, and I adored her. I considered her as a beloved younger sister because there were only fourteen years between us. She loved me in return, and she accomplished the miracle of managing very well a situation that could have been quite difficult.*

Guìa then takes a deep breath and begins to tell me how the story transitioned from one of joy to one of deep despair.

After two years of trying to have a child, she finally became pregnant. Her joy was immense; she felt like a chalice carrying a divine body. She knew she was pregnant well before the doctor could confirm it, because she already knew and loved that soul. But she lost the baby, and in the process had to undergo an operation that ended her dream of being a mother.

> *What was difficult was that no one could understand my grief. When a child is not born, people do not imagine how the*

loss feels. There is not much compassion for a young woman who loses her first unborn child, because it happens quite often. But I had already known my child, and I also had to face the fact that I could not have any more. It was a double punishment, and only my husband could console me. And he did. I loved him so deeply that I knew my pain was not an end in itself. I knew we could live a happy life without our own children. As long as he was at my side, I could deal with anything and accept anything.

Two years later, Caelan's daughter was old enough to express herself freely in front of a judge about wanting to stay in contact with her father, so Caelan finally felt able to divorce without risking the loss of his daughter. He asked Guìa to marry him, during dinner at a fine hotel in London. She does not give me details, keeping this intimate moment for herself. Two months later, her fiancé suffered a heart attack.

Then the horror began. He underwent an eight-hour operation to try to restore blood flow to his heart. He was in a coma for a week, hovering between life and death. I prayed at his side twenty-four hours a day. I told him not to die, not to leave me. I kept talking to him, trying to breathe for him, until he suddenly opened his eyes and told me clearly, before falling back into the coma, "I'm not going to die, because I'm going to marry you first."

Eventually, he regained consciousness. Little by little, some of his strength returned, and he was released from the hospital. The doctors recommended a heart transplant, but he told Guìa he did not have the will to go through it. In the face of his refusal, the doctors gave up on him and left Guìa responsible for administering the drugs necessary for his recovery.

She was twenty-seven years old.

For five months after leaving the hospital, she was alone with her now very sick fiancé, a little girl who trusted her to look after her father, and a big house in a foreign country, far from her family. Exhausted by the ordeal, she finally went to pray in an empty church and made a pact with the eternal.

> *I asked that if Caelan could not get better, that he be allowed to leave quickly and without pain. It was quite selfish, like all of our deeds on this Earth. I mean nothing pejorative by that. I could not imagine ever being happy if he was suffering, therefore it was better for it to end. I thought if he died, I would certainly die with him; our love was so strong that the idea of not following him was outside my perception of reality. So, my prayer was really for both of us.*

Guìa again manages to amaze me. She says what could be considered the ugliest thing with total authenticity. Hearing her speak her truth challenges my beliefs and even my belief system, but I have faith in her and am determined to be open to the truth, no matter the consequences. She doesn't masquerade her actions as charity. She does not need to hide behind altruism. She owns fully doing everything out of her deepest and first instinct of self-interest, in the purest sense of the word. I can see how adopting this point of view would allow for all guilt to disappear from my life. She gives me access to a new level of self-acceptance.

As time went on, a miracle occurred: Caelan's health improved. Although he was still certainly tired, Guìa was amazed at the change that took place. He insisted on choosing a date for their wedding. She did not want this ceremony; she wanted him to concentrate on his health. But he was unshakeable in his determination. Life resumed, and laughter filled their beautiful, love-filled house again.

Guìa and Caelan had a small wedding, attended by the thirty people who, from the beginning of their love, had always given them their full support.

The ceremony was moving and joyful. As they exited the town hall, they stopped to offer Guìa's bouquet in homage to Sainte Thérèse, a favorite saint of hers. They prayed together, and she felt a strong and inexplicable emotion grip him. As he got up, he looked at her gently and told her he now knew what he needed to know, and that everything was perfect. She did not ask him what he meant.

They went on a honeymoon to a tropical island, Guìa worried, her husband insistent. His little girl was now safe, he told her, he had fulfilled his duty to all of his children and his family, and he now wanted to focus on their marriage and their future. He wanted to settle on the island and buy a pineapple plantation. His optimism was contagious; Guìa wanted to found an orphanage.

We spent five magical days on that island. I loved my husband.

I loved being married and bearing his name. I had not known the difference it would make to be married, but it opened a new world for me. It affirmed our love with a statement so public, so universal, that nothing could threaten our union.

They took a car to visit two or three plantations for sale. They were sitting in the back of the car, holding hands silently, enjoying the beauty of the island, the lush greenery and the infinite expanse of turquoise water, when Guìa suddenly felt a freezing shroud fall over her, bringing a crushing sense of doom. She instinctively turned to her husband, panicked. She asked him if he was well and was reassured by his calm response. He told her, looking at her with his big, mischievous, and loving eyes, that he was perfectly satisfied. There were, he said, so many beautiful things to accomplish on this island, that it would become the seat of their love. He could not remember a time in his life when he had been so happy. She smiled with pleasure, reassured, and returned to her contemplation of the beautiful sea.

He died in the next moment, suddenly and quietly, from an acute cerebral embolism. Five days after their marriage, Guìa was a widow. Her seven years of love had been a haven of tenderness.

While understanding the accomplishment of her life had been to dance with both happiness and unhappiness, to live through all emotions, eventually freeing herself from the world of duality, I feel deep regret for her. Sadness washes over me, thinking of how she lost this man whom she has described as the blood that flows in her veins.

Once again, she reads my mind and whispers to me softly.

Everything is always perfect, darling. I had reproduced the cocoon my parents wove for our family when I was a child. I loved Caelan so much I did nothing but delight in his love. I identified with our relationship. Life, my life, was our relationship. I could face all the difficulties, all the malice, all the judgments if I was by his side. I had found my protector, the one who watched over me, defended me from predators, the one who would never betray me, the one who adored me and satisfied me fully. I had abandoned the mission I gave myself at the age of twelve, which was to experience the world. This cocoon-like state could not last if I was to fulfill that intention. Everything is always perfect.

I cannot see the perfection in losing the man you love, but Guìa is at peace, and that alone gives me food for thought. What am I missing? Is the whole of life only and forever just a meaningless series of experiences? Is that all there is? I leave for the day in a state of despondency and bleakness. *What is the point?*

CHAPTER 10

THE TIME OF DESPAIR

After letting me wrestle with the meaning of tragedy, the next day Guìa teaches me about the cost of resisting what is, whether good or bad. For her, refusing to accept Caelan's death renewed the strength of her ego, prolonging her suffering before it, eventually, became a pathway to her liberation. She had to first experience despair as her world crumbled. The following five years were a nightmare.

She found the strength to talk to Caelan's children and reassure them of their father's love. Her husband's death caused all divisions and disputes among his loved ones to disappear and be replaced by love and compassion, and Guìa was proud to have known how to soothe and forgive.

She is grateful that her last words and days with Caelan were loving. She does not know if she would have survived her loss, she says, if guilt had been added to the emotional upheaval. From that moment on, and for the rest of her life, taking a person for granted has never been an option for her. She makes sure to never leave someone with angry words, always underscoring her love for them, which tells her that she is loved in return.

> *Much later in my life, I supported the victims of the terrorist attacks in New York, and the biggest regret most of them had was that they did not part from their loved one with caring words. It was so heartbreaking to witness them having to cope with one of the great life lessons that we tend to forget in the routine unconsciousness of everyday life: do not wait for an emergency or a tragedy to wake up and get your priorities in order. Being right, or busy, or distracted is not important.*

> *We all know this, but how many of us actually put it into action? We all know anything can happen in the next minute, but we live as if this were not so. The cost of surviving is being oblivious to the only thing that matters, to the only thing that can soothe and heal us: love, expressed and demonstrated.*

She made it one of her life practices to complete each of her days reviewing any unfinished conversations to make sure there was nothing she needed to attend to, nothing to apologize for. I know she is challenging me to review the state of my own relationships, many of which I have taken for granted.

Guìa quickly discovered that her husband had put the sole responsibility for his financial empire in her hands. She had addressed this issue with him a few weeks before their wedding, when she suddenly remembered that most wealthy people sign a prenuptial contract before committing to each other. He had laughed, telling her everything was set up, and no contract was necessary. Since he had been completely in charge of the structure of their lives, including the finances, she had not pursued the subject.

I found myself in charge of a large business and responsible for the financial future of my husband's four children. He had everything perfectly organized, but it was necessary to make decisions. His company had hundreds of employees whose futures had to be safeguarded, so it was necessary to conduct the sale of the business with this in mind. I learned to talk to lawyers and bankers. I chose how to divide his assets and distribute them among his children. I still do not know how I did it, but I did it!

One of the greatest sources of pride in Guìa's life is that there was not a single fight over money with her husband's children. She knows her husband would have been proud of her too.

Money, very much like love and sex, is a topic that makes people crazy. So much meaning is attached to it, beyond what it actually is. I had learned through living with Caelan that money was just money—useful, practical, and to be appreciated. But for some, it means so much more. People often measure their worth as a person by the amount of money they have; they measure how much they are loved by the amount they inherit; they deal with their fear of lack by holding onto as much as they can, even at the cost of their relationships. But the truth is, money has no significance other than the one we attach to it, and this can be one of the sources of suffering.

Caelan's children moved away after his death, but they were always respectful and courteous toward Guìa. She was particularly engaged with his second daughter, who had a severely handicapped child yet had created a life of remarkable balance. She juggled a family life of admirable quality with an unfailing devotion to a nonprofit organization in support of children who have this disability.

The many facets of the emotional storm surrounding the loss of her husband did not leave Guìa with much room to breathe. When she was not concerned with maintaining the peace and doing what was fair, she had to deal with the mystery of what happened after death. Was her husband safe? Was he cold? And above all, she yearned to hear of his love for her one more time. She knew the irrationality of these concerns, but in a desperate plea to the unknown, she constantly asked for an answer, though she did not expect to get one. Then, months after his death, in the middle of a long night of sobbing, she got a sign that her pleas were being heard: she saw a light flicker for a few moments in her dark bedroom. There was no logical way to explain this light, not that she cared to explain it.

I knew it was him; I knew he was answering me. I also knew, and I cannot say how, that it was difficult for him to do so, but he had succeeded through the power of love. This moment brought me a lot of peace. The next day, my sister called me to share a dream she had had about Caelan. She told me he was bathed in white light and wanted her to tell me he loved me and that he was safe and well. One has to experience this kind of gift to know the soothing and tender feeling it gives. The intimacy of the connection that takes place during these moments is such that it makes it hard to share with others. I hold it as a precious present to this day.

Sadly, in spite of the sign and of the love of the people in her life, Guìa sank into a devastating survival mechanism, disastrous not only for her, but also for those around her. She knew, even then, that death was an integral part of life, and she knew she could surrender to what had happened, that she had the option to accept her husband's death. But the pain of the loss was too great for her to withstand. So, she did everything she could to avoid feeling, not realizing that this avoidance would cause a vertiginous plunge into suffering.

Guìa explains to me the distinction between suffering and sorrow or pain. Suffering is, from her point of view, optional because it is based on stories we create and repeatedly identify with; we then become convinced that our lack of happiness is caused by those same narratives. Sorrow or pain, on the other hand, is a logical emotion that arises from certain circumstances of life.

I hated everyone because they were still alive, and I blamed them for it. I remember being in a park watching an adorable boy playing and thinking that I would prefer him to be dead rather than my husband. I spent my time raging against God, life, bad luck, fate, my guardian angels, and the world. I had no future to look forward to other than a very long and bleak ordeal.

I considered myself a victim and, therefore, I had no control over my life—since, by definition, a victim has no power. I was like a leaf letting itself be carried by a stream, with no active participation of any kind. I reaped huge benefits from playing the victim, because I got a lot of sympathy, I did not have to act, I focused all the attention on myself, and I did not have to make the effort nor generate the courage to face and deal with my fears. My rage allowed me to feel less pain. I avoided all aspects of life that carried risk. But the other side of the coin was intense and deep suffering, immeasurable annihilation. I spent years just rocking myself back and forth, trying to alleviate the vivid ache that a terrible, black monster called despair was inflicting on me, a monster that was eating my bowels while I was still breathing. All these efforts were in vain.

The death of my husband was the last of several tragedies I had lived through, and it was the straw that broke the camel's back. In this moment of utter despair and resentment at the cruel continuity of life, I drew a logical and necessary conclusion about myself: I was cursed. It seemed the only rational and coherent meaning I could find for everything that had happened. For me, this was just a statement of reality.

Guìa became full of complaints. Complaints against life, against humans, against fate. She became hard and cold, and an icy shell seemed to separate her from friends and loved ones. When a person close to her annoyed her, she would attack. She frightened others. And to make matters worse, the guilt she felt after making a scene, the pain she saw in her targets' eyes, and the fear her anger generated made her feel as if a small piece of her soul was breaking, reinforcing her decision that she was cursed. She would then experience an immense and profound sadness, at an almost spiritual or existential level. This only added to her pain and despair. She lay in a vortex of misery, a deadly cycle in which she created the very thing she was trying to avoid.

> *My life was full of complaints and lamentations. Those whom I considered to be my friends were those who sympathized and, therefore, understood me. I did not like people who looked at me in exasperation and told me to stop the drama. I judged them as selfish or simply not interested in my trials, but in any case, they certainly did not understand what I was going through. My complaints were totally constructed around my need for revenge against life. I had found another way to survive, but this time, instead of being a superwoman, I became a destroyer.*

She took up to six baths a day, because, she tells me, the water seemed to somehow alleviate her pain. The rest of the time, she watched movies, trying not to pay attention to the troll that devoured her heart.

She developed an uncontrollable fear that the people closest to her would each, in turn, die. She called them several times a day, trying to find a way to breathe a little more freely. And the rest of the time, she complained.

Guìa tells me that the perception of a danger is the source of all complaints, in the same way smoke indicates the presence of fire. The perceived threat is often pain, sadness, or something we do not want to accept. For her, it was the fear of losing more people she loved. Her answer to fear was to ontologically kill them by complaining about them, refusing love, and preferring resentment. Her complaints were a protective reaction.

While I pretended not to be the author of my choices, not to be responsible for the consequences of my actions, for my words, or even for my life, I was not aware that I was paying a high price for this destruction, for this denial of responsibility. It had to do with the golden rule of life, which is that one always reaps what one sows. Or rather, one always reaps what one says. I, indeed, collected a harvest of bitterness, suffering, self-centeredness, and desolation, causing the very result I was trying to avoid.

Guìa explains that responsibility does not mean being the cause of something, does not mean being at fault or deserving blame or praise, does not mean something morally, socially, or legally correct or incorrect.

Operating in the realm of victimization involves losing one's power—as, by definition, a victim has none. Operating in the realm of being responsible allows for one's power to arise. Being a victim lets one wallow in misery, while being responsible demands an acceptance of what is and what is not. Being a victim invites emotions like resentment, anger and hate, sadness and regret, while being responsible calls for forgiveness and surrender. The choice is ours.

She uses the word "responsibility" as a context in which to operate, a gift one bestows on oneself to operate in a chosen realm. And she teaches me that there is no relationship of cause and effect between the context and its content: a context gives access to a specific view of life's circumstances. After the death of her husband, she chose to live as a victim, and she paid a heavy price.

Evening is falling, and she is done for the day, leaving me with a battle raging inside me once again.

While all of my life's conditioning pulls me to feel sorry for Guìa's pain and torment, I now understand that she could have avoided it by taking responsibility and accepting what life presented to her. I confront the possibility of taking such total responsibility for my life, and it humbles me.

While walking back toward the village, knowing that branding anyone as a victim is the equivalent of condemning them to a powerless life, I struggle with the dilemma of my feelings for what Guìa lived through. I suddenly remember she spoke to me a few days earlier about the difference between compassion and empathy. I did not understand at the time what she wanted to impart, but it is now becoming clearer. Compassion is knowing what she went through, while demanding the best of her: she could have transcended what she was facing. Empathy is feeling what she felt, therefore becoming myself a prisoner through the identification with her despair. I breathe a sigh of relief as I realize I do not have to be a cold-hearted spectator of Guìa's despair in the wake of her husband's death, but I do not have to take it on, either: I can simply love the Guìa from that time and trust that she found a way out of her struggle. I can acknowledge her power and support her.

I come to the conclusion that suffering can destroy the ego if we are willing to suffer consciously—or, it can feed it if we identify with it. I have always considered suffering to be our biggest enemy, but it might after all be our biggest ally in the evolution of consciousness and the burning up of our ego.

CHAPTER 11

ANOTHER DREAM

After I fall asleep, I dream of a woman in her forties who lives in a community where being aggressive toward others is an accepted game that goes back to the first human societies.

There are anthropologists in my dream who explain that this way of being allows members of this society to feel a little more interesting, a little smarter, and almost stronger than others. They claim members of this society feel safer by belittling each other; sharing the same opinion against someone reassures them and makes them feel part of the group. They, therefore, justify the continued use of complaints, taunts, accusations, and defamation, and they reap a desolate society.

My dream is dark.

One woman, in particular, has an absurd and pathetic complaint about her mother, and their relationship has suffered greatly as a result. The woman's problem is that every day, her mother insists the woman eat fish, convinced that this will make her even smarter than she already is. Her daughter is exasperated by this behavior.

I see the woman in my dream spend forty years blaming her mother, feeling asphyxiated and being dominated by her resentment. This woman blames her celibacy and lack of social life on the fact that her mother has lived with her and always wants her to eat fish. Her anger at her mother has dominated her entire life, and she has become more and more miserable.

Guìa then appears in my dream and tells the woman that she admires the depth of her mother's love. If she were a mother, Guìa says, she would never have pushed devotion so far as to brave every day, for years on end, the rage of a daughter who does not want to eat fish! Guìa explains that this woman's mother loves her so much that she continues to seek enhancement of her daughter's intelligence in spite of the pain that effort causes her.

I witness the disbelief of the woman when she finally hears what Guìa is saying. She has never considered that her mother's position is a testimony of her love. I see the woman walk towards her mother, and I witness the worried look on the old woman's face as she seems to wonder if her daughter is going to attack her. But the daughter takes her mother in her arms and, at last, thanks her for the immensity of her love. The mother then bursts into tears of gratitude: finally, her daughter understands that when she says, "Eat fish," she means, "I love you."

Certainly, the woman would prefer a mother who says "I love you" instead of "Eat fish," but I watch this woman stop blaming her mother for everything that has not worked in her life. In letting go, she is able to feel her love for her mother, for the first time. And at the very moment when this woman gives up her resentment, there is an explosion of sparks of all colors. As if by magic, this community of unhappy people finds itself in paradise.

Before I awaken, a final image from this dream is imprinted on my mind forever. I am in a rowboat with another person. There is a hole in the hull on the side of the other rower, who asks for my help to stem the gushing water. But I say, "Do it yourself. Bad luck for you! The hole is on your side."

I wake up with a start and realize what I did not see in the dream: although the hole was on the other rower's side, I was still going to sink with the boat. Either we would both lose, or we would both win. Our future depended on my choice to help or not.

CHAPTER 12

THE TIME OF ADVENTURE

The next morning, I cannot find my way to Guìa's little house, and I wander around in an uncontrollable panic because I am so afraid I will not see her again. I realize later that she has given me a day to assimilate her words. And as always, she is right to do it. The hours spent walking in circles, hoping to find her, allow me to examine my complaints and understand that they have been ruining my life.

It is only on the next day that I find our chairs arranged in the usual way, as if waiting for us, and Guìa takes up her story.

After the sale of her husband's business, she resumed her studies and obtained a degree. She passed her pilot's license exam to challenge herself, she took an apartment in town, found a job, and made a new group of friends—but nothing alleviated her grief. She found no respite from her sorrow in these activities. Then, one day, she found herself standing in front of a mirror having an existential conversation with herself.

I looked at myself, lean and sad, and I gave myself an ultimatum:

I should either kill myself or find a way back to life. Suicide was not an option, but if I continued to be a victim of the things that did not work in my life, nothing could change. I knew that only when I decided to be responsible for the misery that had invaded my life would I then become the cause of the misery. And by becoming the cause of what was not working in my life, I would then be able to transform my life. Only at that point could I look for solutions.

I took a backpack, resigned from my job, left my home, and traveled around the world. I was hoping to find a way back to life, and it worked. I left behind five years of feeling sorry for myself.

At the start of her travels, Guìa kayaked through the Grand Canyon in the United States, braving the rapids and the cold, sleeping under the stars. She met people who did not know her and with whom she could be normal, meaning she could drop the label of "widow" that burdened her so.

Then she met a friend in Bora Bora and spent six weeks at the seaside, regaining strength through the exquisite beauty of the islands. She swam, bicycled, and walked, until the day a sailboat arrived in the port with an English crew on board. The crew's job was to sail to different corners of the globe for owners who wanted their boats moved without having to do it themselves. While sharing a meal with the crew captain, and without really thinking about it, Guìa told him she had always dreamed of sailing around the world. The skipper immediately said he needed a new crew member and that she could join them in Auckland,

New Zealand.

I think he wanted me in his cabin more than as a crew member, but I decided to be open to what the universe presented to me. I said I would meet him a month later in Auckland. He asked me if I knew how to navigate, and I lied shamelessly, saying I had learned it during my aviation training. The truth was, I always got lost as soon as I took off!

She eventually found herself at a huge marina in Auckland on a fifty-one–foot boat. The job was to sail the boat from there to the Caribbean. She had no idea what it took to cross the southern Pacific or how dangerous such a voyage might be. And there were dangers, because this craft was intended for tourist navigation in calm, Caribbean waters and was not equipped with a radio or a global navigation system. Guìa asked nothing, trying with all her resources to feel a little more alive, to suffer a little less. In truth, the idea of danger was stimulating.

I quickly got used to life on a boat. There were four of us: a couple, the skipper, and me. There were three small cabins, and we had to share the chores, take turns at the helm, cook, and tend to the boat in general. I gave myself over to this adventure.

One of her first times at the helm was on Christmas morning, from four o'clock to eight o'clock. She witnessed the sunrise that day, which, without her knowing it, marked the beginning of her spiritual awakening. She was sad, and she was alone, contemplating the immensity of the ocean. The rising of the sun painted the sky and the ocean with colors ranging from deep purple to the most delicate of rose. She felt her husband's absence profoundly, and her family was at the other end of the world. Suddenly, six dolphins appeared, three on each side of the boat. They accompanied her for thirty minutes as the boat moved across the water, and her heart was soothed.

> *While aware I was filtering reality through my needs and desires, I considered that moment as a gift that meant I was not alone. I connected with the whole universe and let go of control, which allowed me to then experience the most extraordinary adventure.*

She learned to sail the boat in such a way that it would surf the big waves of the Pacific while avoiding the tankers. She learned to watch the whales with wonder, and to meditate before the endless beauty of the ocean. After a few weeks at sea, a storm erupted, with waves so high they seemed taller than the mast. The crew rushed to the deck to furl the sails and lower the anchor in an effort to stabilize the boat. In her haste, Guìa did not hook her safety line to the rail, and she almost fell overboard. She escaped drowning only thanks to the skipper, who caught her at the last possible second.

In that moment, she confronted her own death and faced the scope of her attachments: being loved, being right, being safe, and attachments to her family and her friends, to happiness, and even to her late husband.

She had been blind to the fact that attachments hurt rather than helped. These destroyed her capacity to be, by keeping her tied to the object of her attachment. That object then became a need. Even wanting to stay alive was an attachment. At this moment, she acquired a new clarity of understanding about a life of consciousness and death as part of the wonderful continuity of life.

She describes breaking out of the prison of her ego and getting a glimpse of freedom. All I can do is listen. The notion of death as wonderful is too foreign for me to fully grasp, even when she explains that only by letting go of all attachments can we be fully alive every minute of our lives. She tells me the only real human tragedy is ignorance, un-wakefulness and unawareness, and I want to believe her, knowing there are certain things I can only get by experiencing them myself. I am ready.

The crew of the sailboat waited long hours locked inside the cabin, knowing they were at the mercy of the angry elements. When calm finally returned, they were exhausted. The gooseneck that allowed for the raising of the mainsail was broken, water had entered the engine, rendering it unusable, and their supply of drinking water was a disturbing maroon color. The jib was all they had to propel them to the nearest land, Easter Island. They could only hope their food would last and that they would not poison themselves with the water that remained.

After a few weeks, they succeeded in reaching Easter Island. They were towed by the only official boat on the island into the small creek that was a natural harbor. After several months at sea, Guia was finally back on land. This was the beginning of another new experience.

Traveling with an English credit card and British pounds, I could not buy food at the island's only store with this currency. I found myself at the mercy of the inhabitants of the island.

Now I was the one who received, the one in need, the one who was dependent on the charity of others. Someone allowed me to use their garden hose to shower, another gave me tomatoes and a fish he had caught. After weeks of eating only canned pineapple on the boat, I enjoyed the miracle of water on my skin and the delight of fresh fruit. It was divine.

Easter Island is the most isolated place on the planet, almost twenty-five hundred miles from the Chilean coast. With a single village and no trees, this dusty island of seven thousand people is home to some horses, tomatoes, chickens, fish, avocado trees, and the famous Moai statues.

There were also disturbing caves where, she learned, there had been human sacrifices, plus a small deserted beach and a huge airstrip the Americans had built in case their shuttle could not land at the Kennedy Space Center in Florida.

The nearest place to get the boat's engine repaired was Chile, so after arranging for that to be done, the crew had no choice but to wait on the island until the engine was returned to them. Just as they were settling into island life, a Hollywood film crew arrived, with plans to spend the next six months on the island making a film produced by a well-known star. They all quickly hit it off, giving each other affectionate names, one group being the "boat people" and the other the "film people."

I was still young, free of obligations, and I lived in the present; the future didn't exist for me at that time. I had a lot of fun. I got a job with the director of the documentary being shot in parallel with the film, and I discovered the world of a film crew, which was, in fact, a microcosm of human society—men, women, and children, living and working together. We had crazy evenings drinking local alcohol and dancing all night; beach days filled with playing; long days of filming that were interspersed with laughter and occasional arguments. The men courted me, and I flirted freely and deliciously until the day my temporary employer demanded that I choose between him and all my other admirers—that I stop playing with their feelings, including his.

She laughs a sunny laugh that reflects this spiritual island, where she found a new taste for life. The filmmaker, Liam, was handsome in a manly way. He was good, young, and his inexperience of the hazards of life meant he had no personal baggage to drag around. She chose him.

She tells me he used to take her in his arms and rock her during her nightmares, and judged neither her pain, her moods, nor her sadness, which could still arise suddenly. He was ambitious and sound of body and mind—a fundamentally good person who was passionate about cinema. It was a gift of hope and lightness of heart for this wounded young woman who was, little by little, regaining her confidence.

He was falling in love with me, and it bothered him because, he said, he had always imagined falling in love with a woman during a wonderful adventure after a long, solitary journey in search of his soulmate. I burst out laughing, pointing out one could not hope for a more romantic situation than meeting a shipwrecked woman on the most isolated island in the world, when shooting a film produced by an international star!

After a magical six months, the boat was finally ready to resume its journey to the Caribbean, and the film crew was ready to head home. Guìa decided to go her own way, first to Chile, then to Argentina, and finally, she headed to Los Angeles. Those adventurous months, which were separate from the world but also opened the door to the world, had given her the idea of working in the film industry. She also admitted to herself that the temptation to see Liam again was irresistible. She wanted to find out if life would give her the opportunity to be part of a couple once again. She leaves me in suspense.

On my way back to the village that evening, I ponder her determination to use every circumstance she encounters as a lesson in awareness. I am concerned about the difficulty of a life spent in search of the extraordinary, but there is something seductive in the way she both lives fully in the moment and uses it to have new insights. I wonder if I can train myself to do the same. But I am already exhausted at the thought of what it will demand from me, fully aware of how hard it is to navigate the very thin line between self-centeredness and a commitment to liberation.

CHAPTER 13

THE TIME OF TRANSFORMATION

Guìa's return to normal life, out of the cocoon of Easter Island, was difficult, and she fell into her old habits of complaining in full force. She contacted Liam, but this did not save her. She was, once again, weighed down by grief, like a person carrying a load of wood who is crushed under the weight of it.

It was during this time that one of her friends proposed to register her in a philosophical self-awareness seminar. In three days, she would gain an understanding of the mechanisms of the ego, thereby enabling her to take the reins of her life. That seminar was, indeed, the turning point, a moment of truth. Her awakening, though, did not take place in the seminar room itself, but out in the street.

Inside the seminar room, Guìa's anger and aggression surfaced with a vengeance. She spent the first of the three days shouting at the leader, refuting anything he said, and acting as a heckler. She was finally asked to leave and not return.

The moment of realization came when she found herself walking on the streets of a foreign city at midnight, alone, thrown out of a seminar she had paid for. She realized the consequences of her anger and knew if she did not do something drastic, she would end up a stereotypical old woman with twenty cats—the only creatures able to tolerate her.

She went back to the seminar the next day and begged to be let back in. That commitment triggered a realization, and she had, at last, the breakthrough she needed. If she wanted to be in life instead of waiting for her death in anger, it was necessary to stop once and for all feeling victimized by the death of her husband. She knew she still lived in the oppressive space she had created around his death, and as no two things can coexist at the same time in the same place, she had to find a way to free herself from the oppression. And she did.

"I am cursed" was the decision she made when her husband died. Living her life inside this context was skewing her experience of life itself. Thinking herself doomed, she could not let people come close to her, for fear of bringing them bad luck. She had lived day and night under the weight of that meaning. Freedom came to her when she realized that being "cursed" or "doomed" was only her view of the facts, and not the facts themselves.

When I took responsibility for this interpretation of my life, I freed myself. It was cathartic. "My husband is dead" does not mean I am cursed, does not mean he did not love me, does not mean I have done something wrong, and does not mean God does not love me. "My husband is dead" means "my husband is dead." This is the closest I can get to reality.

I went from being a powerless victim to being responsible. I had chosen to marry a man who had a heart problem and was twenty-six years older than I was. He then died. In spite of all my pain and all my sorrow, if I were given the chance to do it again, I would. From the moment of that realization, I left the world of victims forever, and I regained my power.

By giving up the "I'm cursed" interpretation, I was able to create a context for my life that could hold the fact of his death, a context that gave me a taste for life and allowed me to generate a new future. By creating this new context, my view of his death altered.

I still found it sad not to share my life with my husband, but I did not suffer anymore. There is a massive difference between suffering and pain. Suffering, as I've said, is always optional because it is linked to being a victim. Pain, on the other hand, is our lot in life, as are many other emotions that require no attachment.

This is my next lesson: a single fact can have a multitude of interpretations, and if I believe my chosen interpretation is the absolute truth, I will then enter a world that has nothing to do with reality. Contrary to what I have previously thought, the meaning of things is not self-evident; the meaning of a word, event, or behavior is never set in stone and depends entirely on the perspective of the observer.

Interpretations are only possible through language. As we humans are the holders of language, we have an infinite number of possible interpretations within our reach. It is useless to try to understand, explain, judge, or invent the meaning of the objects of our interpretation, because it is impossible. The objects of our interpretation have no intrinsic meaning. Interpreting only leads to the risk of misinterpretation, confusion, or misunderstanding. The consequence of this is the end of our ontological freedom.

She convinces me that we deceive ourselves when we confuse facts with interpretations, interpretations with truth, and interpretations with what really happened. It is the equivalent of thinking the menu and the food in a restaurant are one and the same thing. The menu listing of small mushrooms on a bed of field greens is an interpretation of the food. To confuse the interpretation with the facts would be as absurd as eating a menu.

She declares that I do not need meaning to live. Merely understanding my interpretation as *my* interpretation and that my truth is not *the* truth will allow me to become open to what is possible. I need only know that I will never have access to the truth, and I can choose my own truth: which means I have no need to prove or to convince or to defend myself. But, she tells me, her truth is no more significant than that of the eight billion other truths pervading the world every day.

It seems to me impossible to live without interpretation. Yet I know wise people have done so, following the movement of life, anchored in the knowledge that while their senses allow them to perceive and deal with the outside physical world, everything real happens inside of each of us.

I cannot imagine a life so detached from all human passions. Still, my question remains: will I welcome a life without strategies, wants, and interpretations? *What will be left?*

CHAPTER 14

A THIRD DREAM

Later that night I have another dream. Guìa's life lessons are so deep and intense, I escape into the unconsciousness of sleep to be able to assimilate what she is teaching me.

There is a young woman in my dream, and somehow, I know that her adolescent memories are painful, bitter, and heartbreaking; in fact, they are almost unbearable. She appears to be about fifteen years old, frightened and alone because she is wanted by the police for the armed robbery of a supermarket, among more innocuous crimes. Facing a certain prison sentence, she is fleeing from her country. Her family is exhausted, not knowing how to handle her transgressions, and they have turned their backs on her.

The girl arrives clandestinely in a new country, where she has to sell herself physically to survive. My mind races ahead. A dozen years later, she has aged but not truly lived, yet she is well beyond the threshold of desperation. She has learned to annihilate all feelings in order to avoid the temptation of suicide. She spends her days sitting on the edge of her bed, her eyes blank, waiting for night to begin. I watch as a good soul approaches, exchanges a quiet word, and registers her in Guìa's seminar.

No one in the seminar can know who hides behind the thick, black hair that falls like a curtain from the top of the young woman's head. Her body is hunched and skinny. She appears old, sick, and suffering, though she is not yet thirty. A dense, black cloud of despair surrounds her. But behind her, though, I see rays of light.

I dream my way through her next days as she gets access to understanding her ego. Her life reminds me of a boat that is upside down, with the keel on the surface and the rigging in the water. As I watch, the boat turns over, rights itself, and begins to operate in sync with the currents, the wind, and the laws of physics. The woman, this newly buoyant craft, forgives herself and accepts her choices. I see her end the desperate, life-threatening destruction of her body, which allows her soul to breathe a little more freely.

She ponders, then decides to go abroad so she can legally apply for the right to work in the country she has chosen as her home. While living in a community of women, she learns the arts of tattooing and cosmetics. She gains a purpose.

Next, I see her returning home, this time with a legal visa. She opens a beauty salon to meet her financial needs, while also practicing the art of tattooing with burn victims, because she wants to give those wounded by fire a face that is not frightening. She calls the government of her homeland to negotiate an agreement to pay for the damage she did, and then she is able to go home. I watch her find her family and get closure for the past.

Deep in my core, I know she is now in harmony with the universe. She governs her life. In my dream, she is forever young and beautiful, and I realize that nothing is unforgivable. I wake up, full of hope.

CHAPTER 15

THE TIME OF TRAINING

I return to our beach haven the next morning, ready to listen with all my heart to what I now see as an opportunity to transform the very culture of humankind. If we can let go of our interpretations, our stories, and our judgments, then perhaps we can free ourselves from survival. Of course, as I patiently wait for Guìa to join me on the veranda, I become aware that desiring freedom from survival is, itself, an attachment: I am now desiring not to have desires! I sometimes feel that I am drowning in all the paradoxes of her teachings.

Guìa seats herself and continues.

> *My release from the prison of survival was so strong and deep, I immediately decided my life should be dedicated to giving this opportunity to everyone. I decided to follow the educational curriculum of the company that ran the seminars and get trained to lead them. I had found my mission: the eradication of suffering. I threw myself into four intense and emancipating years of discovery and awareness.*

She moved in with Liam, and she worked twelve hours a day, six days a week. The training of aspiring leaders was very intense, the goal being to allow them to discover through personal experience the very design of the ego of human beings.

She often stood in front of two hundred people who wanted to free themselves from their ego, although they were still in thrall to it. She had to learn to lead the seminar without reacting, judging, or offering opinions. Her goal was to be a mirror, so that others would be able to see themselves.

> *You know my story, and you can imagine the difficulties I confronted. I was a bossy woman who had built a thick, tight shell around herself, so nothing could reach her. I was capable of attacking others, if necessary, to get what I wanted. My hardness was my protection. My coldness was a way of hiding my shyness. My entrenchment was my security. And all of that had to disappear.*

Guia compares her training with that of a Zen master, in the sense that she had to embody everything she was saying. No one taught her what to know, no one tried to improve her or persuade her of a certain point of view. This lack of transmission of knowledge was the actual key to it all: personal experience was the key to awareness. Nothing got explained as causes—mountains were mountains and trees were trees. She had to look at everything without judgment, and the calming of her mind took time. She had to learn not to be hypnotized by her automatic thoughts, not to let words limit the possibility of life. She had to surrender to not understanding and let go of her desire to be praised for accomplishments. She finally got to the place where she did not know anything, not even who she herself was.

To remove her absurd feeling of superiority, counterbalanced by an equally absurd feeling of inferiority, she was told to clean the bathrooms of the training center for months, until she experienced the joy of serving humanity through contributing to their comfort. She worked as a receptionist and learned to handle clients graciously, with no personal identification to their complaints. She spent days opening and closing the doors to different classrooms, so the noise did not disturb the participants.

She came to understand the holistic nature of the world of service and making a difference. She often spent more than twelve hours a day encouraging participants to continue their education, without expecting anything in return. She made herself follow deliberately irrational orders from one of her teachers, so that she would learn how to obey before she began to give direction to others.

Guia spent hours sitting alone in front of a white wall, trying to answer the existential question "who am I?" and putting herself happily through the agony of the entire spectrum of human emotions. She even acted the role of Tarzan in front of fifty people, to make sure her self-consciousness disappeared and would not interfere with her commitment to making a difference. She recaptured the pure joy of play, the innocence of a child discovering human experiences.

Her determination to help alleviate human suffering was such that nothing was too difficult. And she succeeded. She became a leader in the company. For fifteen years she led seminars for people of all origins, religions, ages, and ethnicities, giving everything she had to help them grasp the unnecessary illusion of human suffering.

Guìa tells me of the lessons she learned about lies and inauthenticity, about sincerity and authenticity. She insists strongly on the power of language and wants me to become aware of its trap.

On the pitfall of lying, she shares the story of a hundred-year-old woman living in a retirement home. Her daughters came to visit her from time to time, hiding the fact that her son had cancer. After months of treatment, he died without saying goodbye to his mother, and the daughters then hid his death from her. Of course, the woman constantly asked why her beloved son didn't come to visit her, and she was pained that he was no longer calling nor caring enough to see her.

In their desire to protect their mother, the family had robbed her of her last moments with her son, and she was also prevented from mourning him. Her daughters justified this by telling themselves that she was too old and too sick to face the loss. They prayed she would die soon, so she would never have to know of it. The whole family was now on guard and disconnected in fear that they would betray themselves.

We lie when we intentionally and consciously intend to hide something from others or from ourselves, whether for malicious or benevolent purposes. The lie creates a confused, muddy energy. The lie dispossesses the person who is lied to of his or her free will.

Each lie has consequences, even if the intention is benevolent. Sooner or later, the truth will come out. The effort needed to remember when and what to say or not to say, to whom, is exhausting and leads to many complicated situations.

Guìa tells me lies are related to our fears, to our desire to protect others or ourselves, and to our unwillingness to face reality. She says lying is the food of our ego, because lying allows the ego to persist and endure. Lies are a symptom of survival at the same level that a sore throat is a symptom of a cold.

The truth must be told with all possible love and kindness in order to care for others' feelings. It can be hard to generate the courage to tell the truth, but it's necessary in order to respect and honor the integrity of human relations. It has nothing to do with morality, and everything to do workability.

She then goes on to make sure I understand the difference between lying and inauthenticity.

Inauthenticity is different from lying, but is not its opposite. Inauthenticity is a lack of awakening and awareness. It is, thus, a state, whereas lying is an action which emerges from the state of inauthenticity. An inauthentic person is one whose choices and actions do not correspond to his or her own Self. The manifestations of this range from a simple lie to the refutation of our deepest values and principles of life. Inauthenticity, therefore, includes lies, but inauthenticity also includes sincerity.

She tells me story after story to illustrate her sayings, and I am fascinated.

Guìa describes to me the hatred and resistance of one of her students, rigidly seated on a chair in one of her seminars. Every time Guìa said something, the student resisted, attacked her verbally, accusing her of the worst intentions, finally calling Guìa "Hitler." In keeping with her commitment to respect the personal dignity of each participant, Guìa did not say anything in response to this insult. Instead, she remained compassionate towards this student who felt so much hatred.

Some six years later, Guìa received a message from the student asking if she would agree to talk to her. This phone call turned out to be one of the most moving moments in Guìa's life.

The student told Guìa she had had a heart attack, in fact many heart attacks, over an entire night. Someone found her on the floor the next morning. She had spent a night contemplating her death, and therefore her life, while she was in extreme pain. She told Guìa that God had broken her heart open so she could finally let love in.

The student added that she had always known, somewhere, deep down in her soul, that everything Guìa had said during the seminar was true. She had known that if she had only opened her heart and trusted Guìa, she could have been free. But she did not. She had rejected wisdom and directed all her power toward maintaining her ego. She now wanted Guìa to know that she was going to have open-heart surgery the next day—and no one thought she would survive it. She wanted to tell her before going into the operation that she knew who Guìa really was. She had pretended not to know. She had been inauthentic to avoid being responsible for the hate she used to hide her pains, and it was now released. The truth had set her free.

> *Being inauthentic is the sign that we are not ourselves, that we identify with something other than ourselves. An inauthentic person is in survival mode, even if he or she does not know it, because the Self is no longer the source of thoughts and actions. The ego reigns. Just as light and colors are synchronized, survival and inauthenticity go hand in hand. Indeed, in a room without light, there are no colors. The contribution of light coincides with the appearance of colors. In our eyes, one does not come before the other. They appear together. The same goes for inauthenticity and survival.*

I understand that lying is an action and inauthenticity is a state. But before I can think about it any longer, Guìa continues by showing me the difference between sincerity and authenticity.

She tells me how a professor working in a large university had talked to her about his career. He had four doctorates, in physics, chemistry, philosophy, and some other subject she could not recall. He had spent his life studying and acquiring immense knowledge, but all to the detriment of his family. He had not taken the time to see his children grow up. His wife had left, and he did not have many friends. He was even in a difficult financial situation, due to his lack of attention to anything other than his research. He studied, always, without ever being able to reach a moment when he was satisfied with his work. He identified himself with knowledge.

Their conversations allowed this professor to realize the origins of his desperate quest for knowledge. When this man was a little boy in kindergarten, one day the teacher asked the students to name the little French guy with a funny hat who had wanted to conquer the world. Instead of saying, "Napoleon," the little boy had, quite correctly by the way, given the name of Louis XIV. Children can be cruel, and he was mocked and called an idiot. The child decided to survive by proving to himself and to others that he was not stupid.

Knowing became the most important and crucial tool of his survival. The problem was, of course, he could never disprove to himself something that was not true to begin with! A wrong answer can never be the proof of someone's intellectual capacities! In realizing that the decision of a five-year-old had been running his life since that time, this man, authentic for the first time, was finally freed of this pointless survival. No longer needing to prove to himself he was not an idiot, he could finally be himself and stop studying.

The mechanism is the same for each of us. This man was a scholar but did not feel like one, hopelessly hiding the fact that he thought he was an idiot. He was sincere when he said he could not stop working. Sincerity is an action that derives from being located in the context of our ego. Sincerity gives the appearance of telling the truth while one is actually in a state of inauthenticity. This man had pretended sincerely for most of his life, unable to do anything other than study, and he lost everything. Freedom came when he told the truth about his fear of being stupid, because he could then get to the source of his fear and make it disappear. Only the truth about identifying with something other than himself, being stupid or being a scholar, allowed him to be free.

I am longing to understand what she means by authenticity. It seems essential to me to differentiate between sincerity and authenticity, since she has just affirmed that sincerity is a caricature of authenticity.

Authenticity is the fact of being and acting in total harmony with our Self. This is also called being aware, meaning being aware that we are aware. Our thoughts and our interactions with others and ourselves are conscious—beyond our personality, our emotions, our senses, social conventions, or our fears—giving us access to being connected to the universe. In order to be authentic, we need to have a deep knowledge of our ego. To achieve this, it is necessary to be skeptical about everything and to question our certainties and beliefs at all times. In other words, it is important to be awake enough to recognize the emotions, reactions, and thoughts of our ego. A transformation can then be generated. The process of a search for authenticity supposes a reflection of the individual on him or her Self. Authenticity, thus, appears as a condition of ontological freedom.

I am not sure I understand everything, and as always, she knows it is time to illustrate her words with her personal experience. She tells me about the end of her romantic relationship with Liam, the handsome man she met on Easter Island.

A year after moving in together, knowing the strength of his desire to succeed in the film industry, Guìa encouraged Liam to stop working and devote himself to writing a script he could then direct. She had the means to maintain them financially, and she was happy to support him in his passion as she continued to follow hers.

After all, love is being willing to support the other in his or her self-expression. A great couple is not two people next to each other, sharing things; a great couple is the harmonious partnership of the realization of both Selves in the world.

She loved the generosity of this man who had chosen her despite the fact that she could not have children, who let her work more than twelve hours a day including weekends, and who never complained. She loved his beauty and laughter, and beyond all, his passion for the film industry, which was his way of expressing his message to the world. Alas, he gradually lost his way.

While Guìa became more and more powerful and successful, he became less and less sure of himself. He used the circumstances of everyday life to justify his lack of creativity and the abandonment of his dream. Liam became a jack-of-all-trades, or more exactly, a personal assistant to Guìa and, oddly, for their relationship. He went shopping, looked after their home, organized trips, outings, and their daily lives; he comforted Guìa during difficult times, was unfailingly supportive ... and completely forgot about his dream.

Little by little, their relationship lost its vitality. Five years into it, she knew the time had come to separate, for both their sakes. It was not in his self-interest to stay with her; she did not have enough time to devote herself to him, and he needed more support than she could, or was willing to, offer.

We broke off our relationship abruptly. I needed a lot of courage to do it. I could not authentically continue to use a human being for my personal purposes, especially one I loved so much. I had to honor myself and our love, our strong bond, which, by the way, never broke. I had to be the source of the salutary shock that would put him back on his own path.

Six months after their separation, he was betrothed to another woman. He was working, and he had started a family. Guìa was glad for   him. She met his wife and created a deep friendship with her. She was proud to have acted with authenticity and, she tells me, life's law of attraction was demonstrated again: their separation had led her to share great moments of life with this new couple, times when a magical atmosphere was created, an atmosphere of connection and intimacy in which no one felt the need to protect themselves against each other. The connection of the three of them made love a reality.

Being authentic allowed me to start walking on the path of enlightenment. It begins by generating the courage to recognize that we are mostly inauthentic, to acknowledge that we are trying to give an image of ourselves instead of being ourselves. It is hard to tell the truth, but this step is essential. It is impossible to lie to oneself and be awake at the same time.

That evening, we go for a walk on the beach in silence. It is not a grim silence, or pensive silence, or reflective silence, but real silence. I stop thinking and am present to life as so much more than a journey from the crib to the crematorium. I stop trying to conceive of reality, and therefore I experience it as it is.

CHAPTER 16

THE DEATH OF THE PHOENIX

Guìa, now in her forties, was taking more and more responsibility in the seminar company, determined to contribute to the transformation of human culture. The intention was genuine but, she explains, its realization was impeded by the company's goal of making money, pitting the rules of capitalism against its fundamentally humanitarian purpose.

These opposing goals created conflict between the company's stakeholders and seminar attendees. On the one hand, the students had near-mystical experiences during their participation, setting them on the path to awareness. On the other hand, they felt pressured to continually participate and bring in new customers with them.

It was inevitable that the contrast between the students' deep and profound self-realization and the demand arising from the company's material concerns would provoke problems and resistance. It was nearly impossible to champion someone's consciousness and be devoted body and soul to their awakenings while also managing a sometimes desperate need to survive financially.

Guìa was always conscious of this dilemma, but she had chosen to accept the existing system until she held enough responsibility in the company to make her voice heard and influence change. It is always, she tells me, easy to sit in the stands and criticize the players at risk on the field.

She rose in the ranks quickly, delighting in the integrity required from everyone involved. Taking part in an adventure that made a real difference to human beings fulfilled her. She had practically no social life, using all her spare time to visit her family, but she loved her coworkers and loved what she did, and that was enough for her. She was fully committed to spending her life doing this work, but then an event occurred that created yet another unexpected fork in the road.

I was asked to do a TV interview in a country where we were suspected of being a cult. Many of the people who participated in the management of the company were volunteers, and it seemed odd to the local authorities for this for-profit company not to pay the people who worked there. An investigation was launched by a reporter, and I was proud to be chosen as the spokesperson, but not for long. The TV channel presenting the program manipulated their findings, showing only two minutes of my two-hour interview and editing segments out of context, in order to create a public "buzz." They managed to present the work we were doing as dangerous, and it ultimately became necessary to end our presence in that country.

Guìa acknowledges that the company made mistakes. There were employees who should not have occupied the positions of responsibility they held. She also admits that having an army of volunteers participating in the running of the company was less accepted in some countries than in others. They would have done better to adapt to the different cultures in which they were operating, rather than using a one-size-fits-all approach to global expansion.

At the time, Guìa had her own ideas about how to structure the company so as to avoid this problem. Her wish was to divide the business into two different entities, very much following the design of human beings: one part would operate powerfully in the material world, acknowledging the need for financial and other structures, while the other part would be protected from the world of the ego, organized as a school entirely dedicated to awareness. This would remove the leaders from the pressure of our world, leaving them free to create programs and courses that would fulfill their intention to alleviate human suffering. But Guìa's voice was not heard.

Despite the hard-won authority she had acquired, she failed in her quest to transform the company. The day came when, without any warning, an existential moment of authenticity affected the core of her life.

> *I was on the phone, and the executive I reported to was blaming me for not doing my job. I realized she was right: not only was I not following the rules, but I was not willing to do the work asked of me. I did not want to work in a company that delivered a message of abundance and joy but did not apply it internally. I resigned immediately.*

The course Guìa had been on for fifteen years came to an abrupt end. It was a difficult choice to live with and a time of deep mourning for her.

Meanwhile, she discovered that the man she had been living with was cheating on her, and had been throughout their relationship, so she put an end to that as well. She found herself once again back at square one. But, in the process, she had mastered the mechanisms that govern human beings and gained a deep appreciation and compassion for others. She also had gratitude for lessons learned, her journey, her life, and for all life in general.

> *I left because my integrity required it. Integrity does not have a direct relationship with morality or ethics. Integrity is what allows for the smooth running and the good functioning of all things on this Earth, physical or ontological. A tree that has integrity will perform well throughout the seasons: it will lose its leaves during the winter, then grow buds in the spring, then flowers and fruit, and repeat the cycle each year. If I destroy the integrity of this tree, by cutting important roots, for example, it will lose its vigor, wither, and probably die. This rule applied to me. If I did not feed my body, it would weaken and be less efficient. If I did not brush my teeth, I would have cavities. If I wrote a check without money in my account, I would be banned from using the bank. If I did not respect my principles and values, my life would not be working. And if I was not aligned with myself, I would not be free.*

Once again, Guia has opened the door to a new world of understanding for me. I realize that I often confuse morality and integrity, and this confusion is illustrated by my actions. When I make a mistake, I automatically plunge into the context of morality wherein I judge myself worthless. I do not have much tolerance for my mistakes because I identify myself with my failures. It is so painful that I have often resorted to attacking others, taking refuge in alcohol, drugs, or work, judgment or thoughtlessness, rather than facing my failure for what it is: a sign that I am taking risks.

On the other hand, when I do not make a mistake, I think I am a good person, sometimes even better than others. Listening to Guìa, I understand that if I made those same mistakes in the context of integrity, they would not have any psychological meaning attached to them. I would simply become aware of the source of my error so as not to reproduce it, or, conversely, the source of my success so that I would reproduce it. No upset. No stress.

Imagine that, one evening, you drank too much and indulged in a romantic adventure with a stranger while you were also in a committed relationship. You would wake up the next day ashamed and swearing to yourself never to do it again. The temptation would be to say nothing to your partner.

In the context of morality, you would judge yourself, and you would be afraid of the judgment of others. Your normal reaction would be to hide what you did. But from then on, your relationship would never be the same. You would no longer be present, because whenever the subject of infidelity was mentioned—in a conversation, in a film, in the press—your guilt and your lies would return to the forefront of your thoughts. To avoid facing what you did, you would either try to think of something else, stop communicating, change the subject, or protect your lie by attacking someone. Your relationship would degrade, little by little. In the context of integrity, on the other hand, you would tell the truth and be responsible for the consequences of your actions, without the need for any justification, and then you would hope for your partner's forgiveness.

It does not take much to see that the world is not working. We are all living through a societal crisis, and I wonder if it is simply due to a lack of integrity at the very foundations of our society. Are we trying to build a world on quicksand while only solid foundations can allow us to build a world that works for everyone? Are we getting exhausted, confused, tired, and angry because of morality?

I examine my own life from the point of view of the distinction between morality and integrity that Guìa is making clear to me. The basic structures of my life are more or less handled. I do not spend money I do not have, I do not borrow more than I can pay back, I drive the speed limit, and I generally respect the rules established by the society in which I have chosen to live. I value the principles I share with many not to steal, not to kill, to respect the dignity of a human being, and many others. I have even created some personal values and principles for myself, such as to always be in pursuit of the extraordinary, to live a life of adventure, and to surround myself with beauty. This level of integrity allows me the possibility of being responsible for my happiness versus blaming someone or something else for the lack of it. I am in quite good shape in that area.

However, Guìa has introduced me to yet another level of integrity in which my word is my Self, in which I constitute myself as my word. When there is no difference between me as a person and my word, life becomes simple because my word is then stronger than my feelings, my desires, or my fears. My word can then take precedence over my ego, my word prevails over reasons, justifications, or doubts. She has given me the access to continually return to my Self.

She concludes the day by coming back to talking about acceptance.

> *My age and experience of the circumstances of life led me to learn to let go and to become aware of the absurdity of resisting what is. All and everything is an experience. Life is what it is. It is not what it is not.*

The years following her resignation from the seminar company offered the chance to implement this lesson. What she did not know was that the impact of the doctored TV show would continue for years, and the reputation of guru—in the derogatory sense of the word —would stick to Guìa for a long time, to the point of destroying much of her opportunity to start over professionally.

I spent my evening wondering how she would let go of that unfortunate circumstance.

CHAPTER 17

THE TANTRIC WOMAN

Like Inanna, the goddess in the Akkadian myth who descends into hell and is subsequently reborn, in the wake of her job loss and the focus of her energies, Guìa gradually released all identifications to which she had attached herself. She had already abandoned a lot, but there was more to come. To embrace acceptance, any attachments had to disappear. She no longer bore as trophies her widowhood, or her inability to have children, or her rape, but she still had to lay down other burdens such as the professional mastery she identified with, her age, her loneliness, her fears and hopes. In fact, she had to let go of whatever she used to fill what she perceived as a frightening void: the nothingness that came from having let go of all identifications. She decided to take a two-year sabbatical before embarking on a new professional adventure, and her priority for this time was to engage in a spiritual pursuit.

> When I resigned, I felt like I was caught by a huge tsunami, a force I could not control, more powerful than anything I had encountered before in my life. That force was pushing me inexorably in a specific direction, and I could do nothing to resist it, nor did I wish to. I felt as if I were guided, protected,

and I wanted to discover this state of being I did not know, this world in which I did not have the need to control everything, this world in which I listened to what the universe wanted of me instead of forcing a result. I wanted to learn to surrender to a divine force. I wanted to discover the intangible.

She began by transforming her relationship with her body. Guìa was tall, and she did not fit the established rules of contemporary beauty requiring women to be very thin. Her eyes were piercing and seemed to attract people's attention like a magnet, because one could sense in them the fire of her soul, the love and the beauty of her spirit. They held the promise of something exquisite. Yet she had not always loved herself physically, and she knew she had to create an alignment between her soul and her body.

This disconnect had grown with the recent onset of menopause, with its whiff of old age that gives the sensation of no longer being the mistress of one's body. Guìa, refusing to act the victim in the midst of this whirlwind, repeated the litany, "It's just hormones," hoping that, somehow, something would derail the inexorable, unpleasant advance toward a heavier and thicker body, toward a change in how others perceived her. But it was not enough. Her attachment to her younger form did not help that natural transition. So, she confided her discomfort to a friend, who suggested she learn to dance the tango to counter the effects of her changing metabolism.

Curious, Guìa went to watch her friend's tango lesson. She was heartened by the sensual and graceful movements of this woman in the arms of an Argentinian dancer, who whispered instruction in mysterious language: "The Achilles heel my dear, the Achilles heel ..."

Once she began taking lessons, Guìa learned that this teacher, like all true artists and masters, could take a beginner and make her a dancer. He was encouraging, understanding Guìa's need for confidence and the timidity that lay hidden under her self-assured exterior. This man had valuable insight into human beings and into women, in particular. He allowed Guìa to pursue a new aspect of enlightenment, in which transformation expands to the physical realm.

She discovered the richness and integrity of having a body aligned with her soul, beyond any looks or attributes, beyond weight or ability. She discovered the power of allowing herself to go beyond the desire to please others. She was surprised to have been caught in the illusion that only physical perfection would allow her this symbiosis with other humans, an illusion that told her, as it does so many of us, that satisfaction and confidence came from her appearance. I am amazed to hear that she could find an elevation of consciousness in something as mundane as dance lessons. But, for her, everything was related to her passion for awareness. She saw an opportunity to let go of her desire to change herself into what she thought she should be. The joy of dancing let her identify her asinine need to please others and answer their expectations, and thereby liberated herself from praise and blame.

In the tango, the woman does not choose any steps or any moves. The man is in control of the dance and must make the woman shine and please *her,* or he will be discarded. Choice is what rules this art: the woman chooses her partner, chooses to let him lead, and chooses to answer his demands, while retaining the power to withdraw when her womanhood and grace are not exquisitely enhanced by him.

It is the man's duty, in guiding all the steps of the tango, to make the woman the queen of this dance, and the woman must abandon herself to his efforts for this goal to be realized.

As Guìa went on with the tango lessons, she learned to move her hips, to walk like a feline, to know the absolute power of women over men. She was thirsty for the fullness and bliss of surrendering to being a woman, with its contradiction, emotions, and feelings. Years of famine and frustration disappeared, to be replaced by joy and play.

Away from the dance studio, she walked with a rolling gait and burst into irrepressible laughter when, waiting for the light to change before crossing the street, she caught herself cocking her hips. She was often oblivious to her surroundings, her attention entirely dedicated to training her muscles toward the flexibility that gives dancers their lightness. In her determination to accustom her body to the angle required by this dance, she even went so far as to wear high-heeled shoes at all times.

She had not expected that something as seemingly innocuous as a dance would allow her to reach a place that had been closed off since she was raped. That door was opening again—old, rusty, and heavy, but still, it was opening.

> *In my thirst for freedom and the extraordinary, this mad hope of being fulfilled as a woman drove me to register for a seminar on sex, intimacy, love, and sensuality as conduits to the*

divine. This is where I discovered Tantric yoga. I was scared to death to try it, but I was also determined to fully own the feminine in me. So, I went to spend a week in the middle of nowhere with fifteen men and women whom I did not know, and I had my first introduction to the discipline of the Tantric art.

The workshop promised to lead her on a systematic quest for spiritual excellence by realizing and fostering the divine within her own body. The ultimate goal was to realize the primal blissful state of nonduality through the union of the masculine-feminine energy and spirit-matter.

I am in awe. I have always thought of Tantric workshops as vulgar explosions of sense and sensation, shared by total strangers in search of entertainment or strong emotions. One more time, I am wrong.

On this Earth, we cannot have an imbalance and experience joy: neither masculine energy nor feminine energy can dominate. The joy and deep satisfaction we are all looking for can only result from the union of the two, regardless of the gender of the person. Masculine energy is dominant and issues directives. It is protective and strong, geared toward action and results. We all have some of this. Feminine energy is like an ocean, with its power and life-giving qualities. Totally fluid and malleable, the feminine changes form and expression quickly, going from dead calm to tempestuous, from beauty to danger, from comfort to rage, all in the context of love. We all possess some of this as well.

One energy allows the other to thrive, to exist, to express light and wisdom, like the land allows the birth of a river with its unstoppable flow, yet all the while forcing it around mountains and reliefs, calling it to hide underground or to plummet through a plain, to finally throw itself into the sea and meld with the whole, all while the land is unknowingly being carved and shaped by the river.

Guìa needed to fully own the two different and complementary energies, instead of continuing to overdevelop her masculine side to deal with the circumstances life had handed her. That was costing her, and she was not willing to let her fear deprive her of her essence. She was now ready to open up to the possibility of being part of a couple again. She let herself feel and own the desire to be accepted and supported in all the splendor of her feminine emotions. She rejoiced in the liberation of knowing that sexual love can be a type of worship in which partners are an incarnation of the divine.

At this point, she blushes a little and tells me that, because of this workshop, she had a personal experience of the divine through sexual fusion. I think she is reluctant to tell me, but she knows I need to understand what she has been through, and she has the generosity to describe it to me.

After the seminar, everyone left except for one particular man. He had broad shoulders and dark eyes, a deliciously sensual smile, almost carnivorous. He invited me to dinner. There was a fire in his eyes when he looked at me. He seemed to want to devour me. He did not hide his desire, and my blood rushed to the surface of my skin, giving it a soft and warm, tingly feeling.

After dinner, he walked over and reached out to her, and with a single word, "Come," he took her to his room. Guìa thought she was insane to go with him, but she could not resist the promise of total surrender and divine communion. Her desire for the extraordinary overruled her mind. In a low voice, this fascinating man mesmerized her with the flow of his words, which kept her disoriented thoughts at a distance.

He told me to trust him. He told me I was beautiful and irresistible in my femininity, and then he asked me to let him make love to me. He wanted only my pleasure, and he promised me intense joy. I melted.

Little by little, in the midst of kisses and caresses, words and sighs, Guìa found herself naked and shuddering before him like one trembles in the warm sunshine after being very cold. Already languid, she allowed him to take her to a wide couch on which she could lie comfortably. She was exposed, and she knew she could now neither escape him nor move, neither of which she wanted to do anyway. She surrendered.

I can relate profoundly to what she is sharing with me, having myself experienced this desire to escape while hoping my lover will not let me. She was at his mercy, fully embodying the contradiction of a woman willing and unwilling, submissive and rebellious, defiant and seductive, denying and calling for, all at the same time. Maybe the painful domination of women throughout the ages has come from the misunderstanding of these paradoxes.

We were both satisfied in the soft aftermath of physical communion. I kept my eyes closed, not wanting to interrupt the moment created by the union with this man who was so masterful with my body. He got up, and I heard him turn on running water. Gently, he lifted me in his arms and carried me to a huge bathtub where we remained entwined for a long time, my head on his shoulder, warm water enveloping our bodies. I never saw him again after that tender night.

She now knew what was possible in love making, and she continued her quest for the divine, comforted and liberated.

I learned that I could choose to give myself. So often I had thought that I could only have one thing or another, I had to submit or dominate, win or lose. But that night I learned to replace "or" with "and." Changing this one little conjunction allowed me to move from a world full of problems to a world of abundance.

I become pensive, attempting to apply to my life what she has just shared, in awe at the variety of experiences she had been ready to have. My last love relationship had been a disaster. The man was lonely, depressed, and medicated. He was always fighting with the world around him. At night, he did not sleep. He had to resign from one job because other people felt insulted by him, and he could not stand the stress. At the university where he taught, he avoided his colleagues because they were, he said, stupid.

On the other hand, he had a daughter who was disabled, and he had sacrificed in order to give her as normal a life as possible. I found this strange, because her disability meant she could never lead a normal life, in the sense that "normal" means "typical." He did not have friends or family. He had destroyed his connection with his country of birth and his people because they had, according to him, no integrity or morality. He was stuck in a parallel universe in which he criticized and insulted anyone who questioned his ignorance of a different reality. It was his only way to survive the hell he had created for himself. He had to blame others and accuse them of what he, himself, was doing.

I now understand that his rejection of authenticity cost him the chance to free himself. His protest that he did not have what he needed to be free was a lie. He could have freed himself, whatever his circumstances. One can always be free without any genetic, social, cultural, or anthropological superiority. There are skiers without legs, disfigured people who are happy and blossoming in love, poor people who are bathed in joy and generosity, parents with many children who still have time to enjoy their lives, elderly people who are very active, people without diplomas who are powerful, sick people who care for others. The list is long. How can people like this be free, but not him? After my long days with Guìa, I now know that we are all able to accomplish what we want ontologically, regardless of the circumstances of our life.

Guìa continues the train of my thoughts, and I note with a little worry that she is now speaking more directly to me, propelling me to the front of the stage, closing off any possibility of escape.

The refusal to accept that we have everything we need to be ourselves is an illusion held in place by a preconceived idea that we are less than perfect. If we believe it is necessary to have either an innate gift to succeed or special circumstances like money, beauty, or luck, then we are no longer the master of our life. The fact is, we are all ontologically perfect, with varying degrees of gifts or strengths. The world has always been and will always stay a reflection of ourselves.

I have learned the lesson well, and I know I have harvested what I have sown. The first step for me to engage in the adventure of a spiritual awakening is to recognize, without vanity or pretension, that being myself does not depend on external circumstances. Whatever the sphere I choose to operate in, my intimate relationships, my family, my communities, my professional environment, my country or the world, I always have the opportunity to be myself. That is to say, to take risks, to consider my emotions as aids to tell me how to go beyond the circumstances of life, to accept the fear inherent in human nature, to generate the necessary courage, and to stick to my course. I have to know myself, to love myself, to respect myself, and to be clear about my values and my principles of life. I am able in all circumstances to be in alignment with myself.

Pretending to be limited, under the guise of modesty or otherwise, is not helpful and is just the expression of our ego. Indeed, only our ego, with its duality of good and evil, better and worse, should and should not—with its suffering and doubts, with its little critical voice—can keep us from being ourselves.

The list of fears preventing me from being myself runs through my head: fear of the gaze of the other, fear of being too small, too silly, not "up to it," fear of being not good enough or powerless, of just not being enough. I know now there are no genes or cells or neurons or anything else that can validate my experience of not being up to par.

I have to admit that these fears exist only in my thoughts, and therefore in my language, because language is formed by thoughts. But now I know I have the power to think and speak differently.

I have indulged in the thoughts telling me I am flawed because, somehow, they have protected me from taking risks. Guìa has made me see that this is a false security. To choose what I think, or at least to choose what thoughts I will give power to, can enable me to realize what I desire. I need to empower the thought pushing me toward the extraordinary and not the one paralyzing me. It does seem easier said than done, but at least now I understand the possibility of it.

You belong to the universe. Listen for what it wants from you. The circumstances of life will no longer be a burden, but will simply be obstacles to overcome, lessons to learn. It's really about going beyond the limits you think you have. Those limits will disappear to make space for something bigger than yourself. If you consider that problems exist in language and are not real, that what is a problem for one person is not for someone else, then you can choose a problem worth your life because you will be free of making problems wrong. This will give you the freedom of choosing what your life is for. For example, when you decide your life's purpose is to save children at risk, a problem like self-doubt becomes inconsequential.

I think of Gandhi, who conceived of the possibility of freeing India through nonviolence. He was imprisoned, beaten, and went on several hunger strikes, but never deviated from his purpose. In fact, he preferred to die rather than give up. I could certainly argue that what Gandhi achieved ultimately made no difference, since India is still suffering. But I know that is not a valid argument, because the possibility he created—the possibility of nonviolence—will always be available to everyone, everywhere in the world. It still seems easier to stay in my comfort zone and justify it by telling myself I do not have what it takes, but now I also clearly understand the price I will pay for that choice.

> *You are not your doubts. You have doubts. You are not your fear. You have fear. The games your ego likes to play will control your life and keep you small if you refuse to be responsible for your identifications.*

I must admit that for the first time, I feel great relief when my day with Guìa ends. With her, I feel trapped in the extraordinary, but I cannot give up my habits of banality quite yet. Guìa is telling me I am a whole and complete and perfect being, but it is a little too soon for me to fully embrace that idea.

I welcome the chanting around the campfire of my village. The children's innocence is soothing. I begin to think that maybe I should reconsider my commitment to engage in the journey to consciousness. Maybe awareness is overrated.

CHAPTER 18

THE REBIRTH OF THE PHOENIX

Feeling rested after a long sleep, I am ready to hear what Guìa did after the Tantric retreat. I have spent enough time with her to know there is more to come, and I am looking forward to it. She manages to surprise me once again.

About six months after the Tantric seminar, a friend recommended to Guìa that she attend a meeting organized by a guru determined to teach Hinduism to Westerners. Having decided to say yes to what life offered her, and because she was always interested in new experiences and new adventures, Guìa went to the meeting. She wanted to learn about this religion, with its fascinating and mysterious ceremonial practices. It was the month of October, a precursor to winter, a season she did not like much. When she arrived at the simple but comfortable hotel in   a small village in the mountains, Guìa found herself in the midst of hundreds of Westerners wearing flowing, white dresses. She laughs as she tells me the story. She recalls her astonishment at seeing all those people dressed in robes and costumes created for the hot and humid climate of India while the meeting took place in the snowy countryside of Middle America. The incongruence of these garments was a shock, to say the least, but she also delighted in the absurdity of it all. She was wearing black.

I still had the remnants of an instinct to rebel, to resist, to denounce everything and nothing, to be different and insolent, and I claimed the right not to love being told what to do. I was there, fully aware of my ludicrous attitude, given that I had chosen to go, but I also loved my distrust. Yet I must confess to buying a huge white shawl to cover myself, out of respect, if nothing else. But what a snub to my professional past! I had been accused of being a cult leader while working in a business, only to find myself now associating with what was almost certainly a real religious cult.

These people bowed and smiled at every human being they met, out of love and deference to their simple existence. But Guìa could not stop her cynical and somewhat suspicious opinions and thoughts from rising to the surface. She was, at the same time, masterful at recognizing her little egotistical voice, the voice that judged and constantly evaluated, and she could observe it without risk of being overtaken by it. She did not know what was going to happen in the next few days, but she was getting used to taking risks and enjoyed the uncertainty of the outcome. She reminded herself that she wanted to continue in her spiritual quest, and above all, she wanted to tame the emptiness of her life, to love, and she hoped to meet the divine. Therefore, she put her critical voice aside, and she played the game.

I found myself in a huge conference room with seven hundred people, with a card on a ribbon around my neck with my name written on it, for all to see. I came into the room with my mind analyzing and judging everything and everyone, including myself; I judged myself for judging! The room was white, the floor was covered with white paper, the stage was white, the curtains behind the dais were white, everything was white. Small white lights were blinking, white lilies decorated the room—everything was white and whiter.

The disciples were completely silent, which favored Guìa's intense inner dialogue that vacillated between comedy and seriousness. Suddenly, everyone in the room turned, as a monolith, toward the front door and greeted with complete, silent fervor a slight, exquisite, dark-haired woman wearing roomy and fluid clothing. She looked as if she were gliding on the ground, with a smile that could have belonged to an Italian Madonna.

The moment my eyes fell on her, I loved her. I felt it as a rolling wave, gentle yet powerful, sweeping my doubts away. And I think the seven hundred other people there had the same experience.

The adulation I felt so instantly is still a mystery to me, but I know that attributing it to a person can be a trap. I think, maybe, a guru only exists inside the space created by the boundless love a group can generate in unison towards an individual. Perhaps the ecstasy of the participants in these religious societies comes from this extraordinary experience of shared love. Anyway, here I was, in ecstasy before this woman. I stayed and enjoyed the experience.

The guru spoke and laughed, loved and teased, as she led a light, but deep, three-hour introductory session that was a good reminder of the priorities of life. At the end of this session, Guìa went to bed.

> *Once I was asleep, I had a dream. It is difficult to convey all of it, but it was one of those dreams in which I was conscious during my sleep. This dream was a gift, a rite of passage, or at least an experience out of the physical realm, and it led me to go further in my search for the divine.*

Guìa describes the dream to me. She was in a beautiful forest, in   the company of the guru. They were walking, and Guìa showed her, with great pride, what she was capable of. Ferocious beasts came to meet them, menacing and dangerous, and though Guìa was afraid as anyone would be, she tamed them using charm and communication. She coaxed them to abandon their hate and aggression, and then sent them on their way, transformed, sweet, and docile.

Continuing their journey, Guìa showed the guru she could manifest love and beauty by bringing forth brightly colored butterflies and birds wearing necklaces of sparkling diamonds amidst flowers, and also by making a beautiful garden appear. Guìa was the source of this magic. With her eyes bright, and feeling self-satisfied in her abilities, she then turned to the guru and waited for acknowledgment.

The guru, smiling, took Guìa by the hand to soften her words and said "This is not enough, my dear. I'll show you what's coming now."

Hands clasped, they climbed an exterior staircase up to the flat roof of a house made of red earth. From there, Guìa could see the entire world at her feet. Standing side by side with the guru, she stood watching the world in all its splendor, peace and war together, beauty and evil coexisting, forming the chaos we all know.

Suddenly the clouds opened up, and without being conscious of any action on her part, Guìa's hands unfolded themselves, palms facing up, and an enormous ray of light came down from the heavens and touched her palms. Under the guidance of the guru, she directed the ray toward the world, transmitting its divine energy. She was being used by something much bigger than herself, and she surrendered to service. Her mission was now clear to her.

She woke up in an ecstatic trance. She returned in the morning to the meeting room as if walking on clouds. Enveloped in her shawl, deeply satisfied, and expecting nothing else, she sat in the body of the group at the back of the room, basking in a miracle of joy she had not anticipated.

> *After a few hours of meditation and speeches about love, truth, and other major issues, the guru paused and asked, "Where is Guìa?" My first thought was, "Someone else in the room must be called Guìa, because she could not be asking for me. I don't know her." But no one got up. The guru asked again and again, and I started squirming in my seat, not knowing what to do, too intimidated to get up and ask if she was speaking to me. Indeed, how could it be possible?*

Gurus, she discovered later, do not have much patience when they want something as simple as a response to a question. She asked again forcefully, "Where is Guìa?"

> *I half rose, stammering, "Are you addressing me?" The guru burst out laughing, and her next question blew my mind. "This dream," she said, "was it not extraordinary?" Who was she to know of this dream, to be aware of having visited me during the night, out of time, out of space? How could she be so happy and constantly laughing? My stunned look made her laugh even more loudly. What knowing did she have access to? I would spend the next year trying to learn the answer.*

The guru signaled for Guìa to join her in front of the room, and Guìa approached under the curious gaze of the people in white. She did not know how to behave, wondering if she should kneel, or bow, or kiss the guru's hands or feet. Her priority was to avoid offending through ignorance.

Sweeping away Guìa's fears with a flippant hand, the guru took Guìa's face in her hands and spoke to her as if she could understand.

> *The guru said, "It's been so long and so many lives since we've been together. The last time was in Egypt. Your frustration is over now; we are together. In no more than a few years, you will speak with love in front of thousands of people and bring your message to them. You will end your life serving as the mother of millions of children. Get rid of this hard energy, leave only room for love and sweetness. I will help you. You are not alone anymore. You have a previous life to complete. Everything will be fine. I will bring you to God, and you will be in its arms."*

Guia was hypnotized by the guru's words. She felt chosen, and she was full of gratitude. At last, someone was willing to know her, see her, recognize her need to make a difference, to serve, and above all, to fulfill her yearning to be fully accepted, from her dreams to her ambitions, from her arrogance to her weaknesses.

She decided to pursue this spiritual path, since she had no other obligations in her life, no work, no romantic relationship, no place to live. So much of her suffering disappeared in this moment of acceptance, so much doubt and fear was gone in the face of the love of another.

Guia was finally heard, understood, and listened to, without any attempt to change or to judge her. That makes me wonder if this is what the world, in its complaints, seeks. She elaborates on this point until she is sure I get it.

> *I had always thought listening was a passive phenomenon, but I discovered that hearing is passive, and listening is very active. My way of listening could be the source of the lack of communication in my life, or it could be the source of communication. Either the ego listens, with judgments, evaluation, and opinions, or the Self listens, with nothing there, pure openness, allowing the other to be reflected in the mirror we then become.*

I am perplexed, and she continues, patient as always.

> *In my survival, my modus operandi was to spend my time doing, pretending, winning, prevailing, justifying, explaining,*

understanding, being right, protecting myself, and avoiding failures. I wanted to accomplish all this without anyone noticing, and very often during a conversation, I spoke to myself while pretending to listen. I was skilled at accomplishing this while giving the impression of listening, because I'd had a lifetime of practice. I had powerful and automatic filters in place. Obviously, this is not listening.

She says that before her experience with the guru, she spent her life in a bubble, very much like the protective chamber in which we put people with a defective immune system. All her senses grasped what was said to her, either by words, expressions, gestures, sight, or smell—but everything came through this filter of protection, deforming it all. She was both protected and imprisoned by it. Her bubble, she tells me, was a constant internal conversation with herself, made of comments and questions.

She laughs and teases me.

Some people have this conversation with themselves aloud, and we call them mentally ill. But if we all put our internal conversations on loudspeakers, we would all appear to be crazy.

I realize that I am doing exactly what she is describing to me. While she is speaking to me, I am questioning myself as I try to understand what she is saying, agreeing or disagreeing, trying to find a solution to what seems to be a problem. I want her to be impressed by me, and so instead of truly listening to her, I speak to myself to try to arrive at some answers that will allow me to accomplish that goal.

I stay silent, and she slowly adds:

> *We cannot logically be thinking of a strategy, of answers, or anything in fact, and be listening to someone at the same time. This is not listening; therefore, no communication is possible.*

Guìa stays silent to allow me to process her lesson. I remember evenings when I've had, perhaps, a little too much to drink, but I've also had fun because the alcohol allowed me to overcome my inhibitions. I also remember waking up the next morning and torturing myself with unanswerable questions such as, "Did I talk too much?" "Do they think I'm too arrogant?" " Are they talking about me?" "Did I monopolize the attention?"

I remember those office meetings during which I mastered the art of seeming to listen while actually thinking of what to say whenever the current speaker would shut up. I remember being preoccupied with giving the impression of being intelligent and being a major asset for the company, but when I finally was ready to talk on these occasions, I usually found that the subject had long since changed without my being aware of it, and I ended up with nothing to say—because I had heard nothing!

I admit to myself that it's been my habit to mostly listen to what I am saying about what others are saying, which is not what they are actually saying! My life has been filled with a multitude of words, but I have rarely been in communication, and have thereby lost the opportunity to have satisfying and fulfilling conversations.

Guìa adds that being in communication produces the experience of what she calls affinity and cohesion, the experience of being connected with others.

If we allow listening to bond us by giving the other person the right to exist, to be recognized and known, the distance between us and the other vanishes, and communication is suddenly not such a mystery anymore. Only then can we really have the opportunity to be together.

She pursues this line of thought.

> *My listening needs to be anchored in nothing, my mind empty of thoughts, released from my opinions, judgments, doubts, and questions. No more bringing everything back to myself. I learned to give a chance to the other by giving up my need to fix and change what the other is saying.*

I understand that I can give reality to people's words, and therefore, to myself. This is what Guìa has been doing with me during our meetings. She renders an image of my words identical to the ones I give, an exact replica of what I am saying, and it is a gift: she recognizes my existence by the gift of pure reflection.

After the meeting in the mountains, Guìa embarked on a new adventure, traveling with the guru to India, discovering the country, working in the guru's organization, getting to know the structures, rules, and also the weaknesses of Hinduism. Those six months were very rich—in humility, in the completion of past lives, and in mastering compassion. That profound and extraordinary spiritual phase opened to her the inexplicable world of mystical phenomena.

> *I had always been physically repulsed when confronted with poverty and disease. One of my main fears was centered around the physicalness of other human beings. My experience in India allowed me to gain closure related to this fear.*

She went to the biggest Hindu gathering in the world, the Kumbh Mela, where over seventy million people gather each year to pray and chant together. The festival takes place at the feet of the Himalayas, in a very arid and poor region, under scorching heat. The Ganges River runs through the stony plains, and there is no vegetation to speak of.

In the midst of those millions of people, sharing tents with strangers, Guia fed thousands of beggars during the day and spent her nights rolling an oily paste through her fingers to get more food ready for the next day.

Sitting on the floor, next to roaring fires that did nothing to alleviate the heat—without speaking the language of the kitchen workers—she felt happy and peaceful. She loved these people with all her soul, thereby having access to the experience of their divinity while also recognizing the futility of the material world.

> *I could have spent the rest of my life singing chants and serving poor people by day and kneading this frankly inadequate food at night, and I would have been satisfied. I was tempted to stay*

there, although I suspected it would not have been enough for me after a while. But there, for a time, during days spent presenting milk and flowers to gods I did not know, I was able to be fully present.

Guìa learned to meditate under the guidance of the guru, who kept her promise that Guìa would meet the divine. After two weeks of meditation and hours of silence, Guìa had the most extraordinary sensation of leaving her body.

It started with a feeling at the base of my spine, and it soon turned into a wave. A powerful energy went up my back, like a beautiful snake. I breathed deeply, so as not to let fear interrupt my experience, and as it moved up along my spine, I felt an immense explosion of love radiating from my heart. I was a channel. The energy then moved to the point between my eyes, and this time the energy was transformed into a kind of laser. I became a cyclops, with this beam sweeping back and forth over the world around me. And then, suddenly, I popped out of the top of my skull, my body left behind. Light as a feather, I climbed inside a column of tender luminescence. I floated without fear or emotion. I was well.

While she was floating in this ascending column, she perceived on her right a group of people around a wooden table covered with folders and papers. They smiled and waved, and she did not stop. The guru explained later it was the executive board of karma, and Guìa did not need to stop, because she had completed hers.

Still going up, she finally arrived at a magical garden where a woman of beautiful radiance, dressed in diaphanous veils, seemed to be waiting for her. This woman was the personification of joy and lightness, and of the feminine. Guìa knew this woman was the expression of Guìa's own divinity. It was a moment of grace.

Smoothly and without speed, Guìa found herself in her body again, with the strange impression that she no longer had a skeleton, that she was held together by energy alone. Surprised, she opened her eyes to find the guru in front of her, instructing her gently not to move. Guìa stayed that way for hours, not looking for answers, just basking in the aftermath of the experience. Later, the guru explained what she had lived through.

> *The skeleton is the seat of all that is solid during our incarnation, such as judgments, fears, opinions, and resentments. All of that disappeared for me for a few hours. The guru confirmed to me that the goddess I met was who we call God, the divine that we all carry within ourselves. It appears differently for different people, as it is an expression of our divine essence. That experience did not change my life, but it transformed the context of my life.*

I find I am envious, not having had such an encounter myself.

During another meditation session, Guìa met her husband, Caelan. While she was once again outside of her body and outside of time, he appeared. The explosion of joy at seeing each other propelled them into each other's arms. This encounter that seemed to last a second has stayed with Guìa for the rest of her life. She radiates sweetness while telling me about it. Through these experiences, she acquired a faith and certainty in what she calls the divine.

> *I discovered that my fundamental essence was innocence, not in the ordinary sense of the term, but in the sense of a mission dedicated to the presence of joy, the very essence of possibility. I was also aware that my life priority had nothing to do with karma, but was a dharma, a service to life. I had something to bring to the universal game beyond my personality. I did not know exactly what that meant, but I had found faith beyond any why and how. I had acquired the certainty of the perfection of all that is and is not.*

Given the profundity of her insights, I think she is going to tell me she chose to dedicate herself to this spiritual quest, but she surprises me again.

> *All these experiences altered how I looked at being alive. I love and will always love my guru with all my soul, but gurus are corporeal beings and must face their humanity like everyone else. Ultimately, hers was difficult for me, and I left. To be a disciple was not my way.*

Guìa had come to understand that she could not be the student anymore. She had to generate the courage to become a leader, in spite of her fear and lack of confidence. She followed her deepest intuition, beyond logic or intellect, psychology or reason. She realized she had to live her life being carried along by what she called "the universal," this divine energy she could not and would not resist any longer.

Her space, as she calls it—and I think she means the space her body and soul occupy on our planet—was nearly clear of her ego by this time, but not quite. The experience of nothingness was staring at her, bigger and deeper than ever, but she knew there was one last thing she had to confront and master if she wanted to make it all disappear: she had to fully face fear.

Guia and I walk barefoot along the shore that evening, admiring the grandeur of the sunset without exchanging words. As she often does, she holds my arm in an affectionate gesture of intimacy and tenderness. I know I will carry this moment in my heart forever. The fulfillment, the quietness of my mind, the perfection of that instant will always be with me.

CHAPTER 19

FEAR

After all the extraordinary weeks spent listening to the story of Guìa's life—witnessing how she drew insights and breakthroughs from every circumstance, admiring her ability to let go of interpretations and attachments—I understand clearly that there is no way for human beings to talk about what consciousness is. Our language is too limited. All we can do is talk about what it is not.

The next day, Guìa obviously has planned something specific to share with me. She is waiting when I arrive, dressed differently, ready to go somewhere.

She wears walking shoes, a large white shirt covers her slender body over khaki trousers, and for the first time, she is wearing a hat. It is a funny, little, crooked hat that has seen much use, and it gives her the young, careless look of an adventurous, free spirit.

So, we walk for hours until we reach the top of a hill. There, six large, flat stones have been sculpted in the shape of low-back armchairs and arranged in a circle. At its center is a fire pit that has clearly been well-used over the ages.

What seems to be a secret meeting place is shaded by magnificent trees encircling the whole area. I feel secure and welcome in this sanctuary. Guìa and I take our seats, the worn stone welcoming the shapes of our bodies. I know the message of this day is going to be different and important.

As I think about Guìa's story thus far and all of her progress, I admire that after her time with the guru, she was still looking for what stood in the way of her liberation. In doing this, she demonstrated a humility I certainly would have lacked under the same circumstances. If it were me, I would have been satisfied to call myself enlightened and would probably have stopped seeking, believing I had arrived somewhere.

Not Guìa. She knew there was no final destination, only a continual coming back to consciousness that included giving up any identifications as they arose. It was not a process for her, it was a way of life.

She starts talking about fear, and after a moment of surprise, I understand why: after her time with the guru, she then had to generate the courage to be a teacher, and courage is only needed if one is frightened. I also know that the knowledge she is imparting to me does not need to be logical: it is her own voyage, with its ups and downs.

> *Throughout my life, my experience of fear varied. It ranged from mild discomfort to deep anxiety, from a simple tingling to a painful symptom, such as stomach cramps. I needed to become aware of the source of my fears to make them disappear.*

She calls material fears the ones related to lack of food, lack of shelter, the danger of wars and epidemics. Ontological fears are based on an illusion created by our ego, like fear of not being good enough, or of being ugly. She explains the link between the two.

If I am in physical danger, my first preoccupation will be to meet my needs and those of the people I love. Being scared of physical danger is, if not logical, at least understandable.

She confirms what I have always known: we have enough resources on our planet to feed everyone, to give shelter to all. But because of a lack of consciousness, we let people starve to death. I am surprised by her use of the word "consciousness" versus "generosity" or "humanity," but when she gets deeper into the subject, I understand. Her point is pragmatic: if we want to avoid wars and conflicts, or starvation and destruction in general, we need to educate people on the possibility of consciousness. But to educate people, they first need to have shelter and food. That is the conundrum we face.

Only when every one of us is physically safe will it be possible to devote ourselves to solving the great ontological, philosophical, and societal problems. Logically, it is in our personal interest to satisfy the physical needs of each human being because then, and only then, can we hope for a world that works for each of us. We are all connected by our human condition, and transformation needs to happen at the global level. To grasp this, people must reach a certain level of consciousness. As long as the ego reigns in our world, with its need to dominate others—to win and make others lose, to be right and make

others wrong—our basic needs will never be globally assured.
Hence, the need to learn about the ego and expose its source:
fear.

To believe in this transformation seems like a pipe dream. We would have to destroy our conditioning, our cynicism, and we would have to give up our refusal to consider it all possible. I can feel it in myself: I am filled with doubts. I am lucky enough not to have to deal with life at that physical level. I am not in physical danger. I am not hungry. I have a roof over my head. In other words, I am available to create possibilities. I can be aware of my environment and of the people around me. I can inquire into the meaning of my life and life itself, both of which are impossible to do if your stomach is empty.

I examine my ontological fear, the illogical and automatic reaction I had in what I now call my previous life, which drove me to destroy what was possible for myself and others, for no apparent reason. I know my life was pervaded by fear: the worry about not succeeding, not pleasing, losing everything, of not being loved, not having my place, of doing evil deeds. The fear I would hurt others, not understand them, not be understood or accepted, the fear of not existing. I was even afraid of my power. The list is endless.

Even though I was mostly unaware of my fears in the routine of my daily life, they were there—and the one that summed them all up, the fear of not surviving, was the driving force. I can now recognize that I was mostly preoccupied with hiding those fears instead of transforming them. My survival was dependent on concealing what I perceived as a weakness, and I now know one thing for sure: survival is very different from living.

Because I know this topic is, for me, the most important of all Guìa's teachings, I am looking forward to what she is about to tell me.

> *One of my greatest fears was of having a bad reputation. That notion could make me act, think, and talk like the rest of the world. That fear could make me give up my dreams, deny my beliefs and principles. I had to eradicate it, and life circumstances soon provided me the opportunity.*

Guìa tried to get hired as a consultant with various companies and was faced with the unexpected consequences of her television interview, recorded many years earlier, in which she had been accused of being a cult leader. She had to face, on the one hand, a categorical rejection of her candidacy under the pretext that she was dangerous, and on the other, being told she was not qualified, even though the extensive training she had acquired was what made her seem dangerous. Her past, her experience, and her expertise were no longer enviable criteria for employment, given the stain on her reputation.

It is difficult to stand against the insurmountable wall of the societal ego, with the cynicism and resignation it engenders, both personally and in our relationship to others. Guìa knew that any refusal to accept novelty and possibility had its source in fear, but she had to find a new strength in herself so as not to get depressed in the face of this rejection.

> *I changed my name, hid my past, and even went back to school to get degrees so I could be accepted in this traditional world.*

I offered to volunteer, I put myself at the disposal of others, so they could have first-hand experience of what I could contribute, but all to no avail. Nobody wanted me. I was frightened that my life was over, this time for good.

With great simplicity, she then gives me her views on fear and its mechanism. For Guìa, fear came just before her ego was created. Her watershed moment happened at the age of two, during the attack on her parents' farm.

It is as if, at that very moment, the experience of fear was just too much for the child I was. In fact, it was overwhelming. I did not tell you before, but I recall a being standing next to me while I lay in terror on the bed that day on the farm in Africa. It was a very tall and powerful presence, and at the same time, that being exuded kindness. I experienced it to be of masculine energy and called him an angel. He told me that I could just be with the fear, let the experience wash over me, but I did not listen to him. I used rage to stifle the feeling of fear. Somehow, it was easier to be mad than to be frightened. It became my way for many years to not experience fear, until the time when being rejected professionally gave me the opportunity to deal with it in full conscience.

I can understand that the refusal to experience her fear became the source of the ego trap she carried with her throughout her life, until she became conscious enough to address it. But I have difficulty understanding the parallel between the incident she lived through at the age of two and her failure to secure a job. I see that both can be interpreted as rejection, but they appear to be unrelated. And though, as always, Guìa seems to know what is in my mind, her answer to my unspoken question is unexpected.

The tool we use for our survival, for our life, is our brain, especially the part of the brain called the cortex.

She explains that our cortex is a prediction machine, comparable to a computer. Very much as a computer stores data, our brain stores all the sounds, colors, smells, and situations we have encountered since our birth. It does this through our senses.

She explains that my cortex has a complete memory of the world I live in, a total memory of my life, including things I think I don't remember. Furthermore, my brain stores everything in order to predict how it should react in situations similar to those I have known in the past.

My eyes widen. Everything becomes clear. This is when I understand the relationship between what happened to Guìa at the age of two and her subsequent professional failure. Of course she felt exactly the same rejection, pain, and fear she felt when she was a child: her brain sent her a signal that the professional rejection was a repetition of a dangerous moment, and automatically, she went into survival mode.

The cortex is useful for dealing with the world, especially if I want to survive. For millennia, it has been programmed for survival, and that has probably allowed for the continuation of the human species.

I can easily imagine our ancestors being more concerned with finding food and escaping wild beasts than engaging in an existential inquiry! Prehistoric humans had a great need to avoid physical threat. But we do not live in prehistoric times anymore.

The dangers I encounter are not physical threats. Once I recognize the automaticity of my reaction, the possibility of choice opens up: I can continue to use my cortex in survival mode, or I can retrain it.

This is the most extraordinary revelation: my awakening can reach as far as to include reprogramming my cortex away from survival and toward living. This is what we call changing our habits, and I can do it with consciousness instead of force.

I consider how rarely I have been really amazed or surprised in my life. I now realize that this is because my brain interprets all new situations according to those I have already encountered in the past. My brain compares the two, then gives me instructions from its database. This is the reason for my mechanical and always identical reactions. It is totally logical that a computer cannot give any answers other than those it is programmed to give!

I remember my far-away life in Paris. Every time I met people I did not know, I automatically tried to put them in a category I was familiar with. I had to find out their intellectual level by asking what studies they had completed. I had to ask about their marital status, sexual preference, and even tried to find out about their social status by evaluating the money they spent on clothing or jewelry or cars. And once I had put them in the box where I thought they belonged, my actions correlated to the level of threat they presented, if any.

Guìa confirms my insight.

> *When I found myself faced with something my brain did not have a reference for, it could not tell me what to think and how to act. Therefore, desperate to quiet my fears, I criticized, judged, doubted, or just outright dismissed what was presenting itself to me. Uncertainty is very difficult for humans to bear because it goes against what we automatically use our cortex for: predicting. The machine blocks and scrambles to find a solution to something it has never encountered. Many of those who have introduced groundbreaking new ideas, who have understood the nature of the conflict between life and survival, have faced persecution and often death because their societies could not find a familiar reference point for their ideas: Socrates, Jesus Christ, Galileo (who narrowly escaped death by denying himself), Abraham Lincoln, Anwar el-Sadat, Gandhi, Martin Luther King, among others. New concepts are hard to accept.*

I realize there is good news in all of this. It is not enough to distinguish Self from ego. I also need to train my cortex to shift from its habit of supporting survival to serving my purpose of living an enlightened life. This isn't just mystical stuff. I can have access to living fully by understanding the nature of the working of the brain!

I start laughing uncontrollably at this idea. I imagine my friends and my coworkers asking me what I am up to, and my answer being, "I am training my cortex." But really, New Year's resolutions are none other than an attempt to do just that, without the help of understanding the nature of the system.

> *The brain will always be a prediction machine, as a vacuum cleaner will always be a machine that sucks up dirt. But now I knew I could train mine to serve me instead of serving my ego. It was not easy, but it was simple. The road to my awakening required an effort, a transformation of habits. Yet, it was possible, because my brain could be freed from its conditioning. I had a tremendous number of tools at my disposal, from meditation to hypnosis, body work, energy work, prayer, and many other disciplines.*

That did not mean she would never be afraid again, but I get what she is explaining to me. She gained the awareness to interpret each situation by being powerfully connected to what was actually happening, versus automatically repeating the decisions of her past.

> *Going back to the employment situation I was speaking about, I had the opportunity to be a conscious witness to how I repeated my reaction to the incident that happened when I was two. I noticed that every rejection felt like a threat to my existence, but the truth was, I was facing nothing more than ignorance or just a mere lack of need for my expertise. I understood that accepting what was happening did not mean making sense of it. I was finally free to be truly present. Arising out of this breakthrough came a deep conviction that the universe was perfect. Going through that difficult time allowed me to discover the physical*

structures in my brain that were keeping my survival in place, and I was grateful. I let go of my past hurt, and this completed the exposing of my ego.

It was a turning point. Once she reached this level of awareness, she was able to be authentically responsible for her feelings and emotions, for her view of life and reactions, for her stories and decisions; in fact, she was finally responsible for the illusion of it all.

We walk back to Guìa's house in silence, with only the lights of the stars to guide us. I have landed in a new world that I cannot fully understand or even describe. I am nervous, and I don't know why. Maybe I can feel what is to come next: the disappearance of everything I hold as real or true in my life.

CHAPTER 20

A FOURTH DREAM

That night, my sleep is very agitated.

I am in the midst of a dark, maliciously animated forest, with strange characters trying to convince me not to believe in something, and yet I have no idea what I should stop believing. It is extremely confusing and provokes a deep anxiety that shakes me to my core.

I am living a kind of existential moment that calls into question the fundamental illusion of reality. It is as if, in a terrible dance of incomprehension, doubts and questions appear and disappear before I can identify them.

I ask the shadow people in my dream to explain to me what is happening, but they keep chanting: "The immensity of life is beyond what you can understand, the immensity of life is beyond what you can understand, the immensity of life is beyond what you can understand."

In front of my eyes, as if I am watching a movie, politicians govern their nations through their own limited personal point of view; teachers teach history, mathematics, and languages through their own interpretations; legislators are similarly mistakenly inventing the laws of our societies based on automatic reactions to their past experiences.

I see parents trying to persuade their children to act according to the parents' own views, without understanding that their children have different ones. I witness misunderstanding, worries, and anger. I observe all human beings attempting to persuade each other that their own individual points of view are the right ones. I watch, with horror, as eight billion people suffer unnecessarily in an attempt to survive.

All at the same time, it is absurd because it is so pointless, and scary because the whole of humanity is confined to a cruel prison. It's pathetic, as well, because all of them have managed to survive very well under the yoke of the tyranny of the ego, and cruel because it has produced the desired result of surviving—which is to say, they have won by losing.

The cage inside of which we operate excludes all possibility of life, of wholeness and joy.

Everyone dreams of being free, fantasizes about a life of tenderness and fulfillment, all while they are suffering. Most are trying to escape this existential cage by divorcing, moving countries, fighting others, having surgery, resigning jobs, traveling, drinking, or even embarking on a search for spiritual escape by deciding to become monks, all to no avail: they bring their cages with them wherever they go.

Everything is based on morality in this grotesque world of duality; the measures are good or evil, right or wrong, true or false, clear or dark, negative or positive. And no one understands that these evaluations are the very glue keeping their ego in place, and separating them from themselves and from others.

I try to scream to warn them; I yell that they are making a mistake, but no words come out of my mouth. I so want them to see that no one has the power to decide what is right or wrong. No one owns or even knows what the truth is. No one has been designated as the ultimate judge. But they cannot hear me.

My dream then transports me to the jungle of Vietnam, where I watch an eighteen-year-old soldier scream as he sees the head of his best friend shattered by an enemy bullet. In his pain and sorrow, the young man massacres an entire village of men, women, and children. I witness his subsequent life of guilt, trying to atone for this by saving as many people as possible while continuing to hate himself.

I can't stand it anymore; I can't find my breath. I am drowning in despair, suffocating, when suddenly Guia appears in my dream. She explains to me that morality creates division and domination, and no one can elect themselves the judge of others. She tells me that there is always a source from which the ugliness we see in human beings is derived. If we would be willing to look at each person's past and understand how it relates to what we are seeing, we would all then know that we are all perfect in our essence.

She adds that the answer is to judge not people, but only their actions.

I jump from century to century, from the time of slavery when it was not immoral for whites to treat blacks as animals, to the present where it is not immoral to raise animals under conditions resembling concentration camps. I can see that what is immoral for one person is not necessarily so for the other, and love is not possible until morality gives way to self-knowledge, until morality gives way to the duty naturally incumbent upon all of us: to be responsible for our actions and the consequences that arise from them.

I then see myself dissatisfied with my life, with my accomplishments and experiences, relationships and circumstances, constantly wanting something else, and I cannot understand why. All I can do is cry. Tears burst from the depth of my human despair; floods of bleakness, broken-heartedness, and desolation wash over me.

I wake up in a sweat, wide-eyed, panting, and terrified. I rush to Guìa's house, even though it is still night. I want meaning; I want hope; I want a way out. The tragedy of humanity is too difficult to bear, and my heart is about to explode.

CHAPTER 21

THE MEANING OF LIFE

She is waiting for me, sitting in the same armchair on the veranda, as if she knows about my nightmare. Her face is devoid of all expression, including love. She is watching me the way one observes a trapped animal hoping for a miracle.

This agitates me even more, and a torrent of words comes out of my mouth, while my mind continues to churn.

It is not possible to tolerate this suffering that has been endured throughout the ages. There has to be a way out. The purpose of all this time spent listening to her cannot have been just to accept the eternal tragedy of humankind; it is too unbearable in its cruelty. I want her to answer me, to show me the way out of it, but instead of saying something that will lighten my panic, she stays silent, letting me face what seems to be an atrocious existential joke.

I begin to speak faster.

The source of my stories, my arguments, my interpretations, and my opinions parade before my eyes in a continuous film, and I voice them to her. I tell her I now understand clearly my need to identify with another in a relationship, my desire to identify with my body or my work, my family, or even my country. I now have access, after weeks in her company, to the realization that there are only effects in our world, and I now know that I have been attributing causes to things in an effort to fill the existential nothingness. I am responsible for the invention of the reasons and justifications I have used to avoid situations that make me feel vulnerable.

As I am talking, my insight becomes more precise: my lack of courage or a selfish disregard for awareness has stopped me from noticing my inauthenticity, while the tacit agreement of our societies—don't mention my justifications and reasons, and I won't mention yours—has made it possible to escape what appears, to me, to be the gaping and deadly boredom of emptiness.

Of course, I know I've been paying a huge price for my use of identification, I tell Guia. I want her to understand I realize that, up to this point in my life, I have renounced ontological freedom, and that has to alter.

I pursue my litany, feverishly, in the face of her blank expression, telling her I can even finally own the incomprehensible experience of weakness that has accompanied me my whole life—the feeling of helplessness to act, the feeling of not having a say, my jealousy toward those who seem to have power and freedom, my lack of enthusiasm, my stagnation, and my regrets. I have even been responsible for making others weak by consenting to their justifications while knowing they were responsible for their actions. I have taken away their right to this responsibility and changed them into victims.

My justifications and explanations, my lack of integrity, my failures, and my weaknesses have cost me the realization of my dreams; I now understand this profoundly. But, I plead, looking at her with despair, there must be something else.

Where is the solution?

Where is the answer?

Is it all for nothing?

She does not smile, does not acknowledge my diatribe. She just starts talking in a matter-of-fact way.

> *My survival was created by identifying with life as a place where people betray me and throw me to my death. The experience of that existential moment—obviously, illusory—was that I was in mortal danger if I did not protect myself from life. My strategies for surviving this point of view were to be a superwoman, to be brave and full of resources. And here is the joke: for my ego to be able to exist, I needed to confront what I imagined to be the danger of life in order to escape it. Otherwise, my ego could not be justified. My life can be summed up simply: I either tried to get away from life by staying alone, or, when I could not stand being alone any longer, I sought impossible and dangerous situations, so as to escape them and justify going back to being alone.*

I already know what she is telling me, and I wait impatiently for her point.

The circumstances of my life reinforced my ego's view of life. I regularly found myself in perilous situations after the attack on our farm: childhood accidents with traumas and cranial injuries; trying to climb a high-voltage pylon to touch the wires, almost losing my life attempting to save a woman from drowning. My school years were spent with the boys and not the girls, so I could prove I was, indeed superwoman. Then, as you know, there was the death of my horse, the rape, the loss of my baby, not being able to have any more children, and the death of my husband.

There is more: I found myself in a war in Sri Lanka, and then in an orphanage in the Thai jungle, trying to make sense of my life. I ended up in the middle of the race riots in Los Angeles, where there were also floods, fires, and finally, an earthquake. I moved from Los Angeles to New York just in time for the attack on the twin towers, and then was in London during the terrorist attacks in the subway. That's a lot for a lifetime. A friend once told me to hope that governments didn't suspect I was the cause of all these tragedies, because I was always in the middle of them. My father asked me not to move near a volcano, because an eruption was the only thing I had not yet survived!

You see, those were times when I could be right about people throwing me to my death; I took everything personally, as if I were the center of the universe, and this allowed me to use my ego to survive alone, against all odds. It took a lot for me to understand this, to be responsible for the view through which I interpreted it all.

There were also periods of intense self-protectiveness, when I did not want to be in life at all. So, you see, I knew I was in a cage, and I wanted to find the way out. I was determined to find the meaning of life, and I looked for it everywhere. You know my life and how much I tried to learn: I freed myself from the desperation caused by the death of my husband by finding out that only love matters. I recovered from the pain of losing my baby by ceasing to ask "why" and abandoning any claim to ownership or deservingness. But where was the meaning of it all?

Changing the place where I lived so many times taught me to detach from material things. I freed myself from my fear of men by studying Tantric art, from my rape by learning to say no, from the weight of my inheritance by learning the value of money. But I did not find the meaning of life.

Being trained to fly helicopters by English navy pilots, who lived only for the thrill of risk-taking, freed me from my fear of death. It was like the samurai who confronts his death before going to fight, so as to be free to die. I gained strength. I still did not find the meaning of life.

Rafting down the Colorado River taught me the power of choice and allowed me to let go of my arrogance. On that trip, I decided one of our very attractive guides had more muscles than brains, until he told me he had studied at Harvard University. He had chosen not to get into the trap of the race for money, because he loved nature. He had the necessary equipment to play in both worlds. I, on the other hand, had only my disproportionate arrogance! My biggest lessons often started with unflattering insights about myself. I learned not to judge people by their apparent level of material, intellectual, or physical success. I still found no meaning.

My sailing trip across the South Pacific allowed me to awaken to the deep beauty, benevolence, and power of nature. I still did not find meaning.

The festival of Kumbh Mela allowed me to love the people there with all my soul and to recognize the futility of material life. Yet, I did not find meaning.

I searched for answers in spiritual or sacred places: Thailand, India, Easter Island. I fasted, meditated, prayed. I learned a lot, and nothing was enough.

I still did not find meaning.

In yet another effort to find this meaning I so wanted, I invented a mission—to transform the world. I neglected my health, my friends, and my family to achieve a certain level of mastery of the mechanisms of the human being. I conducted seminars across the world for thousands of people, and this experience gave me the key to accepting the ego and discovering the Self.

It was, finally, on an ordinary day spent with friends that I came to my liberating moment. My friends were arguing with each other about something I cannot recall, and I became the observer. I found myself in a sort of trance, conscious, but detached from all passions. I heard their speaking as simple noises, watched their gestures as a meaningless dance, observed the emotions in their facial expressions, and I became a spectator of what the ancient Greeks called the human tragedy: all of life was a play. I finally understood it all.

There is no meaning to be found, neither on the Earth, nor in any action, nor in any place, and especially, not in survival. Life is empty of meaning. The immensity of life is beyond any meaning I can come up with.

My life had been absurd, an illusion I made real, and it felt as if I had come full circle, back to the starting point of my survival, back to that night in Algeria, years ago, when I was still present to being the whole. I was back at the beginning, to the moment before I made up that I knew the meaning of life.

I was free, and I was left with a simple truth: What is, is. What is not, is not.

This is a knife to my gut. I think what she is saying is horrible; life will have no point at all if I accept what she is telling me. I say so, in no uncertain terms.

She laughs.

> *You are adding a meaning to what I am saying. "Life has no meaning" has no meaning!*

I am startled. She continues:

> *I was constantly trying to reach a place where I would, finally, be in fullness, like you are doing now. I told myself, one day I will be known, one day I will be rich, one day I will be slim, one day I will succeed, one day I will be happy, one day, but not now!*

> *But where was I going, pressuring myself so much? Where was this magical place where everything was perfect?*

> *There is no place where we will all be beautiful, tall, strong, intelligent, rich, and satisfied. My survival was a scenario that was based on an illusion, and that had no meaning.*

> *There was nothing to repair in me; I was neither broken nor deficient. There was nothing to change. I was neither less than a boy, nor a monster, nor stupid, nor cursed. Life was not a place where eight billion people wondered how to kill me. I had started my life with an illusion and had ended up with an absurdity. When I awoke to this truth, I finally stopped running.*

The only meaning of my life is the one I give it. The author of this meaning is either the adult I am, or the child I was. I can choose which it will be. The universal law of attraction is unavoidable: you always reap what you sow. Life is about experiencing, and it does not mean anything.

Not only do I not speak, I do not want to. I do not think, either. In fact, I do not do anything.

I am in a nothingness I have never experienced before; it is uncomfortable because it is unknown. Every single feeling and emotion I have ever had has been mine. They have not been given by others nor do they exist in any external reality. I have all the power.

I can never figure out the meaning of life because the immensity of life is far beyond what anyone can ever imagine. Giving meaning to life and holding that meaning as the truth is the path to suffering: all identification with something inside or outside of myself is a trap.

I am no-thing. And everything is possible.

Life is life, is the closest I can get to reality. I have to accept the mystery of creation: I know that I cannot know; I know consciousness as unknowable.

The miracle is, of course, that inside of this context, I can create whatever meanings I wish to, as long as I continue to know that none of it is the truth. I can be the source of my life.

I am stunned. I stay that way for the longest time, remaining present and basking in the experience of being. It is as if my past has disappeared, or rather, the weight of my past has left me, and my future is a blank page. Empty. New. Where everything is possible. I am fully responsible for my life, as I have always been. I have recaptured my free will.

Softly, Guìa pursues her lesson.

> *Every life is unique. Mine has been tragic and adventurous. Others could be intellectual, dedicated, spiritual, or even athletic. The important thing is to follow your path, because we are all looking for the same result: the liberation of the Self from the ego. We are seeking an awakening to awareness so that we can experience consciousness.*

I absorb what she is saying to me at a whole new level, beyond ordinary understanding. My metaphysical interrogations—*who am I, where am I going, what is the meaning of my life, why am I dissatisfied*—do not matter anymore. In fact, even Guìa's mystical experiences do not mean anything; they were what they were. I can now understand the matter-of-fact way she shared them: for her, she never had access to the truth because she could never possess the truth. The truth seized her. My next insight surprises me, as I become present to the possibility of peace for our planet. If there is nothing to strive for, there is also nothing to fight over. I look at Guìa in wonderment, and she gives me the sweetest smile—the most delicious, the most tender, divine smile— before gently adding:

> *The other side of something is something. But the other side of*

nothing is everything.

I remain nestled in this new silence, a silence created not by absence of speech, but by conquest of presence, an eternal and infinite silence, a silence of truth. She has gifted me enlightenment, and I have the ability to evoke the entire universe.

We are the eternal presence.

CHAPTER 22

EXISTENTIAL BOREDOM

How to live a life devoid of meaning?

For the first time in years, nothing is a problem, and my life is a blank slate. I have time to think, but of what? I have time for everything; I know that "eternal" means no time, as in timelessness, but I do not know how to bring things into my life. I do not know how to live without passions, needs, goals, or strategies. It was so much easier to be preoccupied with things and to be stunned into action by reaction.

I can see how fruitless it is to think of anything as significant. I now know fighting against something negative means robbing myself of the positive, as the two always go together, until acceptance robs them of their significance, and they disappear. Everything is unfolding just to unfold, like dancing is just for dancing, or playing is just for playing.

Guìa, ever patient, addresses my moment of uncertainty about this unknown realm with gentleness.

> *Like you do now, I also had little tolerance for uncertainty. I used to pretend I could control my life, that I was in charge of it*

and that death was optional. My first insight after my moment of enlightenment was that it was the opposite: life is uncertain, but death is a given. And I did not know when it would occur. I had to learn to dance with life as things happened, and my role was simply to not make it mean anything. Very soon thereafter, I had to confront existential boredom.

I exhale softly. My nagging question about how to manage the nothingness is not so odd after all.

Existential boredom comes from the paradox of putting oneself at a distance from the busyness of life while being in life, aware but not absorbed by the bliss of consciousness. For Guìa, the sacred gift she possesses is the power to create using her free will. Once she became aware, she could authentically create her life as she wished, and she explains the process to me in stunning fashion.

As I told you many days ago, my tool for creating is language. Using language, my first step in confronting existential boredom was to make a distinction between choosing, which belongs to the realm of awareness, and deciding, which belongs to the world of survival. I did not want to repeat the same mistake and find myself trapped again. If I retained the same meaning for both words, I could not navigate easily between the ego and the Self. Knowing there is no truth and no intrinsic meaning to any words, I found that making that distinction allowed me a lot of clarity.

Obviously, she had not chosen to survive, and neither had I. I cannot pretend I consciously told myself at a young age that I was going   to spend my life being inauthentic and suffering. But I had not been *unconscious* either, in the sense that most people use that term, because I had a say in the matter. For Guìa, our fabric, our essence, who we are is consciousness itself, and unconsciousness is consciousness without awareness. She also calls it a state of perception without awareness.

She proceeds to explain herself further.

> *Deciding is always linked to emotions, tastes, reasons, desires, logic, comparisons, or fears. We evaluate, reflect on the future consequences of a selection, make lists, ask for advice, and select on the basis of what seems to be the most important external factor. In doing so, we kill all the other alternatives and imprison ourselves under the guardianship of the very thing our selection is based on. We lock ourselves in our own trap.*

> *When I decide, I am confronted with various problems, the first problem being that I am not my emotions, my tastes, my comparisons, or my circumstances.   I have them.   If my selections are based on what I can call the circumstances of my life, I give my power to these circumstances, and I become their puppet. My emotions change all the time, my tastes and my reasons too. And so do the circumstances of my life.*

> *If my selection is based on things in constant movement, all I can do is follow that movement. I am no longer in charge of my life, and I become the victim of the circumstances.*

In my life as I have told it to you, if I wanted to be free of survival mechanisms, I needed to retain my power. To be master of my life, to create my life, I needed to be the source of it. This was only possible if I did not decide on one option over another, or for one reason in comparison to another; it was possible only if, instead, I chose. Therefore, I needed to learn to choose based on nothing, and then my choice could include everything.

I still do not grasp fully what she means. To select freely beyond reasons or considerations is too novel an idea. Guìa anticipates my resistance by expanding her explanation.

If the cortex works by tapping into the past to know how to act in the future, thereby creating a deadly repetition of the same patterns, all I needed to do was tidy up the archives of my past. Having emptied my future of my past decisions, I would put myself in front of a blank page onto which I could write an open future. Everything was possible in and with language.

I notice she is speaking in a different style. At first, our meetings were filled with her stories, with the sharing of her experiences. She has now brought me into a world without interpretations or meaning, where the transmission of her discoveries no longer requires illustration. She is asking that I, too, think of myself as a writer in front of a blank page or a painter in front of an empty canvas, to throw myself into the void without any reasons or considerations.

If we think the role of language is to describe the world, then we will be in the viewer's position forever. From that position, the world is there and here, and we can only report what we observe. We live in a model of life where our words fit and adapt to the world. In that case, our only option is to survive it.

I am trying to grasp what she is saying by applying it to my life, and it is quite a revelation. I realize that my default has been to talk about myself and others as objects I can describe with almost physical qualities. With the conviction of fact, I have said things like "I'm strong" or "She is a procrastinator," "he is kind," - "the world is bad," or "life is beautiful," as if everything is fixed without any malleability. I have been the source of rigidity of my world.

However, if we adopt the view that the world, others, and ourselves arise in language, then we end up being the source of what is possible. We then have the opportunity to have a world that adapts and adjusts to our words.

I get it. Language creates a future that did not exist before the speaking of it, a future that alters the course of our lives forever. This language is independent of any past event or circumstance, of any interpretation. This language allows me to create from nothing. And then, everything is possible.

I am feeling elation and awe. I am so very grateful someone has cared enough to explain to me the simplicity of the mechanism of human beings.

I leave Guìa to rest, and I walk along the beach, my shoes in my hand, until I cannot resist the call of the warm water. Quickly undressing, I walk into the ocean, feeling the movement of the water on my body, the vastness of the sky above me, not as outside of me, but arising with me: I am one with the universe.

PART IV

THE GRACE OF CREATION

CHAPTER 23

THE GAME OF LIFE

Leaving Guìa for the night is getting more and more difficult. I would love to just lie outside her door, even on the floor, listening to her breathe, as a servant would do for a much-loved master. I would not do this as a subservient gesture but because I have the need to express my devotion. I know, though, that this can also become a form of attachment, and therefore I never ask to stay with her. Our exchanges during the day, our shared meals, our walks, and our laughter fill me with joy and have to suffice.

It is a bright, warm morning, and Guìa is radiant, wearing her white robes with grace.

She continues to explain to me her way of seeing life.

> *The survival game is to pretend to be what we are not. It includes the whole notion of drama, in which the actor always tries to persuade the audience that what they see is real. The cosmic actor plays with all his heart, to the point that he ends up believing his playing is reality.*

We play this game as if our life depends on it. Every form of progress we have ever made can be considered a game. From slavery to respect for human rights, from monarchy to democracy, from life based on the word of honor to one based on legality, from the inferiority of women to gender equality, from the exploitation of children at work to universal education, all are societal games. They have birthed conflicts, wars and revolutions, suffering and celebrations. For example, "Being rich is more important than being poor" is a choice and not a truth. The artist who thinks he cannot create without despair plays a different game: "Being poor is more important than being rich."

I am starting to get this and begin enumerating in my head some of the games I have played: "Being married is more important than being single," "Being thin is more important than being fat," "Being a victim is more important than being responsible for my life." I realize that when I compare one thing to another in this way, a scale of value automatically arises that creates opposition, and I forget that this valuation is not real. A woman who has been abused by her husband may believe that being single is far superior to being married; some societies believe being fat is desirable to thinness because it conveys material prosperity; and as I have learned from Guìa, I know that it is possible to believe that being responsible for my life is more important than being a victim.

Consider that surviving and living are two different games. Living is only within your reach if you accept that you are the creator of your life. On the other hand, surviving implies trying to be who you are not, meaning you believe you do not have a say in the matter of life.

We are the only species on this Earth that plays this game. If you observe human beings, you will notice we always want to be different, do something other than what we do, or have what we do not have. You have never seen a crocodile going down the river saying, "I wish I could lose some weight," did you? Or a giraffe wishing she were shorter?

She laughs, and I laugh with her. I think about the time I have spent wishing that my ex-husband was more romantic, regretting not having a different employer, hoping for a more affectionate father, dreaming of a different mother.

I remember the money I have spent trying to have another body, a bigger, more beautiful, more luxurious house. I remember the time I have spent resisting what happened in my past, the times I have tried to be more loving, stronger, more disciplined, more intelligent.

I am dizzy with all the "more, better, different" of my life. I even remember looking at my thirty-year-old body and telling myself it was not my body, it was my practice body, a rough draft, and one day, my true, goddess body would appear. I just had to do more of that, less of this, and differently, while trying a little harder, and I would make it.

We laugh so hard as I share all this with Guìa, recognizing the absurdity of the trap I have been stuck in, very much like a hamster running on a wheel, hoping in vain to get somewhere.

Our laughter is becoming a metaphysical experience. I seem to be carried higher and higher by waves of infinity until I am weightless. We cannot stop, and tears flow with the cascades of mirth. It is as if we are dancing with the angels in heaven, as if we have discovered the existential joke we ourselves invented and then forgot.

Each image we evoke revives our hilarity, and Guìa continues her merciless descriptions of the trap we are in.

> *The woman with straight hair wants curly, the ones who have curls spend hours making it straight. Tall people want to be shorter, the short ones wear heels; spouses dream of being free to have amorous adventures, singles dream of being married; children want to leave school while adults dream of studying again. If we are too active, we dream of being able to rest. If we find ourselves bored, we aspire to work more. If we are young, we cannot wait to be an adult, and once we are there, we wish we could be as carefree as a child.*

Pearls of laughter cascade from Guìa's mouth. Her eyes are bright with merriment and joy. We have to catch our breath so she can continue.

> *The inescapable rule of the game of survival is that we forget who we really are, and the consequence of this forgetfulness is that we spend our life searching outside of ourselves for the source of wholeness. No sane human being would choose survival if he was conscious of his divinity. The outcome of the game of survival is a deep, existential suffering.*

I know the hollow void she is talking about. I have tried to fill it with food, alcohol, sex, clothes, by accumulating material wealth, having relationships, seeking success or knowledge. Of course, none of it has ever worked.

Guìa goes on.

> *It is possible to play another game—the game of being, the game of living. It is time for a new culture for humankind, a culture of oneness, awareness, and consciousness. You can choose to define yourself as the victim of life, or as life itself.*
>
> *By reaching a certain reflexive consciousness, we become aware of being aware; what we thought was real becomes only an agreement between us. Symbols become secondary: money does not mean wealth, pieces of papers are not money, green lights do not mean go, numbers do not represent quantities, and articles in a newspaper are not the truth.*
>
> *When something exists, it is a function of relationship. We are mutually necessary to each other: there is not a separate you. Self implies others, life implies death and vice versa, white implies black. Everything is interconnected in an eternal game with no purpose other than what is happening. When we know we are the cloth of existence itself, reality is bewitching. The universe becomes a celebration of existence.*

These certainties are like warm sea water, washing over me. Guìa concludes the day by giving me a treasure.

Here is the most beautiful of secrets: the game of life is the only one you can never lose.

She rises gently and tenderly runs her hand over my hair before pushing open the door of her home. Before she disappears inside, she adds:

My darling, let me wish you a delightful time playing in nothing, where you are everything.

She has pronounced the place at which I have arrived. I sit for some time, not wanting to break the magic of the day when my dear Guìa opened the door to consciousness for me. I think about our conversations with delight and wonderment. Her presence has given me the opportunity to be at the source of my life. I know under her gentle influence, I can only rise toward awakening.

I savor the fact that she came out of the past-present-future trap to be only in the present, and I know it is possible for me too. Her language allows her to do this, and as does mine. We can create a future. But it is not a future of "one day I will get there," it is a future of "now": a future that arises in the moment that we speak it, not lived yet, but real as a possibility, in the moment of its creation.

She is, in fact, like Merlin the wizard, I think to myself with amazement and delight: she has lived backwards from the future.

CHAPTER 24

THE RETURN

I wake up the next day at dawn. The attraction of sleep has faded so much in light of Guìa's magical lessons. I am longing to know what games she chose to play for the rest of her life. I skip on the path to the little house as a young woman would rush to see her first love.

But something has changed.

Soon I become aware I am not on the same path I have used for months. I do not recognize any landmarks. The noises of the animals are different, the insects avoid crossing my path, and even the trees seem less majestic.

I can feel panic rising, fear clamping my mind, my breath catching in my lungs as a primal scream forms in the pit of my stomach and comes out in one last, longing, desperate call to the universe: *Guuuìììaaa!*

But I know. I just know. She is gone.

She had to move on, so I can pursue my path away from her influence. It is up to me to seek new discoveries. She cannot do any more for me—no one can. Nobody can give me the gift of awareness, only the doorway to it. I want to mourn the loss of our closeness, but I have learned that I do not need to. I fall to my knees in a silent prayer of acceptance and gratitude.

EPILOGUE

I was never able to find the way to Guìa's little house again. I never heard where she went or what happened to her, and in fact, I did not need to know. Guìa, woman among women or goddess of the Earth—I still do not know which—had come to talk to me. And now she was gone. And it was my turn to live.

I stayed in Africa, not far from the place I'd met her. Little by little, people came to me looking for shelter, food, sharing, or learning. I opened a large sanctuary for people and animals, where we grow our own food and support each other. And every night around the campfire, I tell my story of Guìa.

I have honored her wishes by writing about our meetings and sharing with others the insights she revealed to me during those marvelous days in Africa. My life is now spent throwing caution to the wind and mostly doing what I love, honoring what is possible. I cannot mourn what is past. Life is all and only an experience, and to tell the truth, Guìa is with me every step of the way. I know we are connected beyond time and space.

You and I, my dear reader, may meet one day, to laugh and cry while sharing our own experiences of struggle and adventure. If not, keep in mind that if one person managed to remember the way to the realm of consciousness, then we all can.

Keep in mind that one always reaps what one sows, and please, do not forget to worship the elegance of the simplicity of this universal rule.

I wish you much courage and love.

By the way, my name is Cecile, which translates to, "the blind one." My name is my constant reminder to never take anything for granted.

GLOSSARY

Awareness:
The space of the mind in relation to which objects of consciousness, such as thoughts, can be distinguished.

Cerebral cortex:
The outermost and most recently evolved segment of the brain.

Consciousness:
The original source of being, constitutive of all things, self-referential and expressed through the brain-mind awareness.

Creativity:
The manifestation of something new in a new context.

Duality:
The quality or state of being in which two things are in opposition with each other.

Ego:
The sum of all our identifications.

Free will:
Freedom of choice undetermined by a cause.

Identification:
A person's sense of association with someone or something.

Mystical experience:
An experience of consciousness beyond the limits of the ego.

Ontology:
The study of the essence of being.

Ontological survival:
The attempt to exist in spite of the illusory nature of a danger.

Paradox:
When something is what it is not and is not what it is.

Physical survival:
To triumph over a danger of physical death.

Self:
The subject of consciousness.

Survival (also see ontological survival):
Continuing to exist in spite of real or illusory adversity or danger.

Unconscious:
The dimension where there is consciousness but no awareness. Also called perception without awareness.

INSPIRATION

While the story of Guìa is entirely my own creation, I would like to acknowledge some of the creative thinkers, philosophers, psychologists, wise mentors and thought teachers who have inspired me. I have read them and made some of their discoveries mine, even when I could not own the totality of their ideas.

This list is not exclusive. I hope the wisdoms of their work will inspire you, on your search for a path to enlightenment, as it did for me.

In alphabetical order:

Albert Camus

Albert Einstein

Anthony de Mello

Antoine de Saint Exupéry

Amid Goswami

Alan Watts

Barry Long

Barruch Spinoza

Cioran

The Dalai Lama

Dan Millman

David Deida

David Hawkins

Deepak Chopra

Eckhart Tolle

François Chang

Frederic Lenoir

James Redfield

Jidu Krisnamurti

Louise Hay

Matthieu Ricard

Michael A.Singer

Osho

Richard Bach

Sai Maa Lakshmi Devi

Jean Paul Sartre

Socrates and the ancient Greek philosophers

Thich Nhat Hanh

The philosophers of the age of enlightenment (XVIII century)

The Bible and Jesus Christ teachings

The teachings of Buddha

Vladimir Jankelevitch

Werner Erhard

ABOUT THE AUTHOR

Sophie McLean is eminently respected for her innovative ability to deliver challenging new perspectives designed to create a shift in paradigm. Her interest is in the nature of being human. She draws on philosophy, linguistics, ontology, and transformation to lead forward-thinking conversations designed to maximize awareness.

Sophie has over twenty years of experience exploring the nature of mind, body, and soul. She also holds two master's degrees in philosophy and is trained as a mediator. She has led seminars internationally for more than eighty thousand people from diverse social backgrounds, ethnicities, and beliefs.

GO BEYOND THE BOOK

Continue your journey with teachings from Sophie McLean.

Visit www.sophiemclean.com where you will discover Access to Awareness: a series of practical programs comprised of one-one-one sessions, workshops, and conferences designed to liberate you from the constraints and the illusion of the ego.

You can also follow her Access to Awareness page on Facebook: www.facebook.com/smc.mclean

The Elegance of Simplicity

Book Cover Design:

Designer: Jacqueline Leak, Paula Donbrow

Photographer: Cleo Sullivan

Book Editor: Angela Houle, Nancy Osa

ISBN 978-1-7329738-1-7

Made in the
USA
Middletown, DE